Welcome to the Family, Jessie

Zoe Quintero

First Edition

PAGE PUBLISHING, INC.
New York, NY

First originally published by Page Publishing, Inc. 2019

ISBN 978-1-64544-634-7 (Paperback)
ISBN 978-1-64544-636-1 (Digital)

Printed in the United States of America

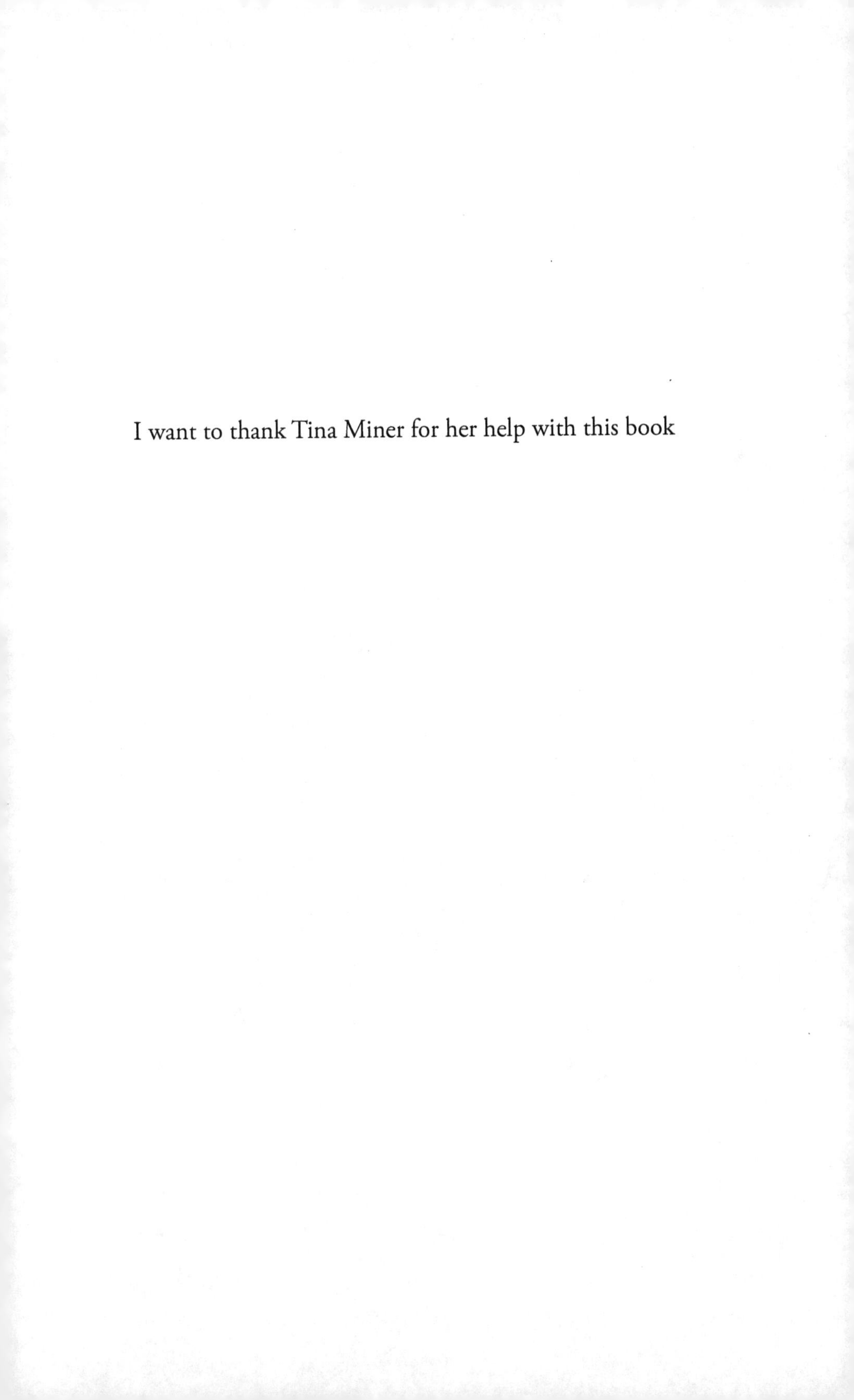

I want to thank Tina Miner for her help with this book

Contents

CHAPTER 1

What is love? I know that it's difficult and can make you work harder than you ever have in your life, for sure. It can make you do crazy things that you have never done or ever thought of doing before. It can also get you in big trouble too. But it can also make you care about someone else besides yourself. Or it can fix you or even fill that big empty hole in your heart. My big brother, Daniel, had something missing in him. 'Til he met that blond curly-haired, blue-eyed girl named Jessie Smith.

Jessie is a sweet, honest, motherly kind of woman, and Daniel is lucky to have a girl like her. She keeps him on his toes, keeps him out of trouble, makes sure he doesn't get hurt, and lets him know she cares and loves him every single day. She's the kind of girl that I want and the kind of girl that my other brother, Matthew, needs.

But she's only Daniel's perfect one and only one, which reminds me that their wedding is in five and a half months away, which is on May 26, 1988, if you wanna know, and everybody is try to make everything perfect for them. Jessie's been finding decorations, food, and drinks for the wedding and doing everything to create the wedding of her and Daniel's dreams. She seems to be a little flustered and in a rush all the time now.

Our dad, who's happy and excited for Daniel and Jessie, told me that she is trying to get everything done, organized, and perfect and that it was in a woman's nature to do so. But everything seems done, organized, and perfect to me. But then again, I'm a guy, so I don't understand woman problems.

Dan and Jessie have been together for about three and a half years already, although it seems to me that it was yesterday when they first met each other. We were playing football, and she was reading her book by the fountain, and we started to tease Dan when he fell down right in front of her and started to get hot and sweaty. But let me tell you about how it all started, how it began, the beginning of our sweet, loving family that grew by one.

I remember walking home from school because I missed the bus again. The reason I missed it is I was having trouble getting my locker open and getting my stuff together. Not only that, but the whole gang went to their homes to drop off all their stuff. So I was walking all alone on a street where I was vulnerable to the rich kids who lurked on the concrete road. Shielded by their Mustang. The gang walked with me for a little while but had to take a different route to get to their own house. But if the gang or at least some of the members of our gang who still went to school came with me, I would be fine because a small group of rich kids aren't going to mess with a bigger group of low-class kids. Probably because we're tougher than them and they know so. Mostly because we get into more fights and get locked up most of our life's that we live in horror and hatred by others who shape us into our rotten selves and make our hearts cold as ice, and our souls black as night

The gang is the group of guys who are pretty much part of our family. They've been there for me and my brothers during the hard times and the good. No matter whether they're risking their own lives. The gang is made up of big, muscular, and tough kind of guys who have hard, tough lives, like any low-class kid. And like most low-class kids, they've lost a lot of blood relatives in their life. But the people in a gang seem to stay a lot longer than some blood relatives. A lot of relatives seem to leave without reason or regret. They just don't seem to care. Then there's relatives who don't want to leave but have to or they'll put you in their own jailhouse. So they leave to live in a jailhouse so you can live in a real house. Then there's relatives who don't have a desire to leave or have to leave. Whether it's fair or not for them. They just leave because it's their time to. Which hurts the most because these relatives are the ones who really do care for you and you know that because they're the ones who actually stayed. But that's not the real reason why we're called low-class kids. We're called this because we don't have well-paying jobs or some of us don't even have a job, so we don't have a lot of money unless we rob stores or rich people's houses. Most of us don't get good grades or live in a nice neighborhood. See, low class. But I will admit, it isn't all that bad, besides being stalked by rich kids then getting jumped by them. But besides that, it's not bad, in a way. I can't really explain what makes it not that bad, but there's something that makes it great. Maybe it's because you have true friends or you don't have to live your life on the line or worry about getting robbed because you have nothing a thief can steal besides your cold heart that weighs ten tons or your loyal pride that's locked up tight. But whatever is good about being a low-class kid, it's sure something no one else has freedom of.

I will say, one person who's had a rough and hard life is John. He lost his true love in a car accident, and his dad left him and his mother when he was still in her belly. John hates his dad for doing that to his mom and him. He left them with no money, no home, and no love. Just cigarette butts and beer bottles. John told us that if his dad ever came back to them, he was going to beat the crude out of him. But that was after he actually met his dad. He was sixteen at the time, I think, and his dad came by his mom's house to see him. But what his dad didn't know was that my parents were there to defend John and his mom. When John's dad tried to get close to him and his mom, my dad quickly got on his feet and said "Leave them alone!" very slowly. At first he looked like he was going to leave, till he turned around to go hit John's mom. But my dad grabbed him and threw him to the ground. Once Dad had his arms behind his back, he said "Call the cops, Anne" to John's mom. After that, he never saw his dad again. Mostly because he's been going to jail ever since and is out of the state.

But the saddest thing is that John's family doesn't want anything to do with him or his mom, Anne, which is just cruel. Only because they believed all the lies and rumors that his dad spread around. But my mom and dad, who have known Anne for the longest time, didn't believe him. They knew that she wouldn't do all those things he said.

So they helped her get back on her feet and helped raise John while raising Dan. And that's how we know John.

John's the same height as my dad and a year younger then Dan. He has light caramel blond hair that's combed into a teddy boy hairstyle. He has honey-green eyes that are very tough and hard-core looking. But really he's just a big teddy bear once you get to know him. In fact, his nickname is *the Bear*. We gave him that name when he grabbed a rich kid and threw him four feet in front of him when he was fifteen. But he did it because that rich kid was pushing Alex around when he was ten. So John picked the kid up (who looked about his age) and threw him to get him away from Alex. He pretty much takes Alex as his little brother. So of course he's going to protect him.

David is a year older than Matt, so he's eighteen going onto nineteen. David is the only one of our gang members with a tattoo on his arm. But he never meant to get a tattoo. It's just that he got drunk that night he got it, so he woke up to find a creepy tattoo on his arm. His tattoo is a skull on fire that's being held by the devil. But the only part of the devil you can see is his hand that's holding the skull and his beady eyes behind it in the shadows. He shows all the girls his tattoo, even the high-class girls. But they usually give him a dirty look and then walk away, leaving him all bummed out. Or they slap him and say, "Get the hell away from me." But David doesn't mean no harm. He's *the Lover Boy* who goes crazy for girls. I mean, once he sees a pretty girl, he's bouncing off the walls in a heartbeat. I swear that he needs a girl under his arm so he doesn't lose his mind, going crazy for all the gorgeous fish in the sea. But at least he acts tough around us or tries to. Until his lovable icy-blue eyes catch a cute girl walking and he's gone in a flash and right on her tail before we can stop him. David has long black curly hair that is crazy messy. He has joyful, lovable icy-blue eyes and is six feet, one inch and buff.

I remember when we first met David. He was a sober fourteen-year-old, passed out on our couch. When I saw him lying on the couch, I grabbed a pan as quickly and quietly as possible and held it like I was getting ready to hit a baseball. I put it above his head and slammed it as hard as I could then ran to Mom and Dad's room as fast as I could, yelling, "I got the bum on the couch! I got the bum!"

They looked up at me when I stepped in their room and yelled "What!?" as they sat up. I nodded at them happily, proud of myself for what I did. Dad looked down at the pan that I was holding in my hand and asked, "D-did you hit him…with…that?" pausing and pointing at the pan. I looked at it and nodded, still happy and proud of myself.

Dad burst out laughing, while Mom gave him a death look, saying, "Stop laughing and go check on the kid. It's not funny, Daniel," then gave him a light slap on the arm. He looked at her and got out of bed, laughing all the way down the hall. Mom and Dad told me that they picked him up that night, when he was getting busted up by rich kids. They didn't know anything about him, and he didn't know how he got to our town or what even happened. All he knew was that his head hurt.

But one day he remembered why he ran off and got drunker than a hillbilly. It was because his parents were fighting again and were going to put him in a boys' home, because his dad was going to jail for stealing money from a tiny store, and his mom didn't care about him, so she was going to leave and go find a new place to live far away and never coming back. David told us that his parents were druggies and that he couldn't stand living with them, so he left and got drunk and lost and the high-class kids were up to no good and also drunker than hillbillies, and that's how Mom and Dad found him after their anniversary, getting the crude beat out of him.

After that, David became one of our gang members and never drank again. Not only that, but his dad got out of jail when he turned seventeen. Yeah, David was madder than hell, but he couldn't stay mad at his old man. But now his dad is a better man after five years.

Now Alex is different from David and John though. He's just a bit more of a gentleman. Not to say that David or John can't be gentlemen or that they're not good guys or that they're not ladies men. It's just he knows how to talk to women. I don't know what he does or how he does it. But he's the *Magic Man*. He can talk to any girl or woman, even if they are a bunch of hotheads.

Alex has always been there when I need him and is the kind of person I can trust. Alex and I have known each other since kindergarten, and we have been friends ever since we escaped those big bullies who were older than us and tried to beat us up. After that, we've gotten into a lot of trouble together. We've made a lot of promises to each other, but the most important promise we've made to each other is we won't get a girlfriend until high school. Now we're in high school, and we still don't have any girls, but I don't want a girlfriend right this second. I want to wait for a while. I don't know if Alex wants to, though. Just by the way he talks about them. Especially this one girl he's been talking about so much. I think her name is Miley.

Alex is five feet, eight inches tall. He has longish black hair that's combed into a long fringe hairstyle. He has eyes that are so dark brown that you can barely see his pupils. He's a few weeks older than me. He has no siblings. It's just him, his mom, and his dad. I would hate it if I was the only kid. I would probably get lonely and bored. That's how he feels, lonely.

He doesn't care if they have a baby, whether it's a boy or a girl. But he already knows what he would do if it's a girl. He told me he would treat her like a little princess and make sure she's always smiling. And if it's a boy, he would make him a good boy and make sure he stays out of trouble. Alex would make a good big brother. I mean, Dan gave him that advice just in case his parents do have another kid. He told Alex to "treat her like a princess and keep him out of trouble," and that was it. One day when I went to Alex's house, we overheard his parents talking about having a baby. When Alex heard the word *baby*, he squealed like a girl inside. I looked at him, and he had a big grin on his face, so I guess he's excited to have a baby brother or sister.

Then there's the Jackson twins, Mark and Clark. Or we can call them *the Ying Yang Bros*. The reason we call them this is that Mark is the bad brother, and Clark is the good brother. Now they might be twins, but they are the total opposite of each other. Mark drinks and smokes; Clark doesn't. Mark shoplifts, and Clark doesn't. Mark doesn't go to school, but Clark does. Mark wears black leather jackets and boots, while Clark wears plaid shirt with vans. Mark goes out with every girl he meets, and Clark only goes out with Lilly. So I guess this means just because two people look exactly the same, doesn't mean they like the same things or do the same things or act the same. I met the Jackson twins when I was five years old. Once I saw them, I was freaked out. I had never seen two people who looked the same before. Until I met them. I mean, they have the same marble-gray eyes, the same light-golden blond hair, the same smile, the same everything, even the same nose, and it freaked me out, and I didn't know what to do.

So after I stood there staring at them for a few seconds, I ran as fast as I could to Dan, screaming "Ahhh! Monsters!" all the way to him. (Dan was eleven at the time.) Once I got to him, I hid behind him. He gave me a worried look and asked "What's wrong, Mike?" as he turned his head to look at me.

I pointed at them and said, "They're monsters!"

Then he looked up at Mark and Clark, who were looking at us. Mark waved at us with a big silly grin on his face, while Clark stood there, scratching his head like a confused monkey. Dan gave me an angry look and said, "They're twins, Mike," and everyone started to laugh at me. Dan had to explain what twins were to me. It still kind of freaks me out sometimes that they look the same, and it also makes me mad too because sometimes times I call Mark, Clark and Clark, Mark.

Bradley and George are also brothers. But they're not twins. Bradley is eighteen, and George is fourteen and a half, but George looks like a ten-year-old. It's probably because he's so small and has a childlike face shape. So we call him *Boy*. He didn't like it at first, but he learned to love it. But I think George's height and childlike figure has some advantages. Like he doesn't get hurt during a rumble. He doesn't even get one scratch on him. Which doesn't come as a surprise to us because not only is George a lot smaller than us but he's a lot smarter than us too. When it comes to school, he is. He gets all As all year long. But he's even more smart during a fight. He's like a little boy who's a secret agent or spy, because you never see him coming. That's one thing about George; he's small but smarter than hell. Some might say that it's the big, strong guy that wins the fight. But it's really the smart one because he probably knows where to hurt them. Bradley isn't that smart, though. But he knows how to kick some heads in. He knows a lot about fight and all the removers and fighting techniques. And to think, he only learned them from his television. He likes watching a lot of action, horror, or any movie that has some kind of fighting in it. Like *Darker than Amber* or *The Delta Factor* or *The Executioner*, movies like that. George doesn't like those kinds of movies. In fact, he doesn't like very many movies. He's more of an outside person.

Bradley has reddish-brown hair with a little bit of strawberry-blond streaks in it and is combed into a long hair pushed back hairstyle. And just to top it off, he has slick satin-gray fox eyes. George is the same, but his hair is a little bit lighter and is combed into a thick businessman hairstyle, and his eyes aren't so slick but more of a gentle sugar-gray color. Bradley drinks and smokes like Mark, but not as much. So he pretty much drinks a little drink and smokes a little smoke.

One time George asked him why he does. But Bradley didn't tell him why. He just told him not to do it and made George promise he wouldn't. George is a good promise maker. You tell him not to tell, he won't tell. You tell him to do something, he'll do it. All the low-class girls are always trying to get him to do something for them. He tries to tell them no as politely as possible, but they keep begging him anyway. Then we have to go save him from a bunch of hoodlum girls who try to get boys like George to love them and turn the boys into delinquents. But like usual, David tries to pick them up like they were doing to George, and like usual, they turn him down.

As I was walking, I started thinking about what my grades would be after taking those long, boring tests a few days ago. And I wondered what my dad would do if they weren't good grades. My dad is always strict with me but never with my brothers, Matthew and Daniel (or you could call them Matt and Dan too). He is especially easy on Dan, though. It might be because Dan's older, and he's already graduated, and he's more responsible than Matt and I.

Dan is twenty-one years old, a man now. He turned twenty-one last month. The one thing I don't get, and it's really sad at his age, is that he doesn't have a girlfriend yet. He told me he works too much and too hard to have one. Although Mom told him before he moved out of the house that "work doesn't make a man out of you, it's a woman that makes the man of you," but he probably wasn't listening to her, or maybe he didn't understand what she meant. So he probably didn't get the point, because he works and works till he can't work anymore and has to get a day off. But now that Jessie and he are together, he doesn't work as much. They split the bills half and half.

But anyway, Dan is six feet, two and a half inches tall. He has aquamarine eyes that can look right through you if your lien or play a trick on him. His hair is cut in to a graduation hairstyle. Except it's a bit of a thicker graduation hairstyle than the usual graduation style. His hair is a really dark dirty blond with a few light dirty blond streaks in it. As far as I know, he's the strongest, tallest, and the oldest in the gang. He's pretty much the leader of the gang, probably because he's muscular and more serious than the rest of us, but not as serious as our dad.

Dan is the kind of guy who is big, big like a bull and strong like one too, but not mean like one. When a high-class girl sees him, she thinks he's like any low-class guy: rough, wild, unmannered, a hood, a punk, all those things. But Dan is different from all those things. He's big but sweet. Strong but gentle. Kind of like that bull from the book *Ferdinand the Bull* that our mom used to read to me when I was younger. That's the kind of guy Dan is. Hopefully a girl realizes that sooner or later.

Now Dad is like Dan, you know, big, strong, muscular, all that, but isn't quite as gentle or sweet like him. Dad is always yelling at me about everything I do. He tells me how lazy I am and how I should do football or track or any kind of sport so I can get a scholarship. But the only time I want to play football is when it's for fun, and all I want to do is read books and finish school. But he doesn't realize that I want to do what I want to and not what he wants me to do.

Dan and Matt are always telling me that he says this because he wants me to have a better life and do things he wasn't able to do. But shouldn't he support me on what I want to do?

My dad is six feet, two inches tall, a little shorter than Dan. He has pure hazel eyes that hold anger. His hair is up in a graduation cut, kind of like Dan's. Besides his is thinner and not to say, his hair is dirty blond with a few gray hairs in it, only because he's forty-one years old. Although he's still pretty muscular like Dan, with a wide chest and broad shoulders, which makes him and Dan a lot bigger and stronger looking.

But Matt is the whole opposite of them, besides being strong like them. But he is not as strong as them. He's six feet exactly. He has light blue-brownish eyes with a little bit of a darker line around them. His humble eyes seem to make people go crazy, in a good way though. Like, it makes them want to have nonstop fun and just be wild. But I will say, his eyes aren't always humble. They can turn naughty once they catch a cute girl eyeing him. His hair is a light brown with a little bit of dirty blond in it and is cut in to a fagon hairstyle. Matt will turn eighteen in a month and a half, and I swear the older he gets, the crazier he is. Well, at least when it comes to girls.

He and David are really crazy when it comes to girls, and I mean crazy. Especially David, he goes bananas for girls. But when Matt smiles, his handsomeness outnumbers David 100 percent. Matt's smile can make you smile and make all the girls fall in love with him and want to be with him all the time. Although when they get to know him, they think he's a child, even if he's just being funny. But they seem to fall for that handsome face of his, and don't forget that bright smile of his either.

Me, on the other hand, I don't pick up girls like Matt or David, and I am not strong or tall as Dan. I'm the whole opposite of my brothers and Dad. Besides the looks, you can tell that we're a family by what we look like. But you can't tell the difference between us until you get to know us. I'm not crazy like Matt, but I do look a lot more like him. At least that's what everyone tells me. I'm not as big and strong as Dan, but I am responsible like him, unlike Matt, who can barely clean his room without being told to. I have light dirty-blond hair that's combed into a messy professional hairstyle. I have blue eyes with a little bit of brown in them. I am five feet, ten and a half inches tall. I'm fourteen years old going on fifteen in about two more weeks. And for an almost-fifteen-year-old kid, I'm not so muscular like other low-class kids. Mostly because I read too much and watch too much television, at least that's what Dad says. But I'm not weak or fat. I can still fight in a clash with the gang and take a few punches.

Our mom, Kennedy, was forty when she passed away. She was the one thing that kept us together and kept Matt out of trouble and me from fighting with Dad and Dan. Well, Dan didn't really do anything. All he did was play football and do his best in school. Mom used to call us Danny boy, Mattie, and me, little Mikey. We never let anyone else call us the nicknames our mom gave us. Not even dad. When they did, they would tease us. This one time, Bradley thought it was a good idea to call Matt, Mattie, all day. Once matt got tired of it, he punched him and said only mom can call me that, asshole. Bradley never called him that again. Especially after our mom died. In fact, no one called us by our mom's nicknames again. But now she isn't here with us because cancer got her, and she died two months ago, before any of our birthdays. Her very last words to us were "Stay true to yourself and kind to others. Continue your life without me, but no matter what, I'll always be with you boys." I still remember those tears that slid down the side of her cheek as her head started to rest peacefully on the pillow and the sound of fast beeping in the background. We sat there knowing we couldn't do anything about it. It was painful to watch my mom, my own mom, die in front of us. It was hard to let her go. It seemed that now that she was gone, we were all broken. Like she was the sweet, joyful glue that kept us all together. We were lost without her, like leaves in the wind.

Our mom was the most beautiful woman in the world, and there was no right for her to die. She had dark brownish-blond hair with bangs in the front. Her hair was pretty long too, now that I think about it. She had hazel-blue eyes that shone like stars in the night sky. She was five feet, five inches. She was skinny and curvy. She was sweet and thick like honey. She would always treat me like a baby. Probably because I am the baby of the house. When she was alive, Dad was a lot nicer and liked to have fun. But now that she's gone, Dad is now the opposite of nice and doesn't like to have fun anymore. Dan says it's because the one person that he loved in the whole wide world is now gone. But I think I'm the one who took it the worst when she died because I ran away and missed school for a week, and let me tell you, everyone was looking for me. The police, the gang, my brothers, my dad, the whole town in fact. But I didn't know where to go because I've only been out of town a few times, and I didn't pack any food also. So I just decided to go home. Once I got home, Dad started to go off on me like a ticking bomb, and that was the first time he ever yelled at me, when Mom died.

But anyway, as I was walking alongside the curb, thinking about those stupid tests I took, I heard the screaming wheels of a car behind me that came out of nowhere. I turned to see what was going on. It was the high-class kids going around a sharp corner with their flaming Mustang being retards. But then I noticed that it was Chris's car. I could tell he had about four or five friends in the car with him too. I got this feeling in my gut that they were going to mess around with me then mug me, like they tried the last time. Although they didn't get to mug me because my dad, brothers, and the gang came just in time.

They haven't messed with me since. But maybe they were just waiting for the perfect time to mess around with me and beat me up. As I watched them get closer and closer, my heart started to pound faster and faster, probably because the last time they got me, they were just about to mug me. Until my dad grabbed Chris by the T-shirt and threw him, and my brothers and the gang started to chase them back to Chris's car while throwing rocks and sticks at them. But I guess that didn't scare them good enough, because they zoomed right in front of me and stepped out of that black Mustang painted with red, orange, and yellow flames.

Then Chris said, "Well, well, well, what do we got here?" He was walking slowly toward me.

"A little punk, Chris. That's what," Chris's friend Ethan said.

"Oh, do we now?" Chris said, pulling out his switchblade.

All of them started to chuckle as they got closer and closer to me. So I stuttered, "You better stay away or my dad and my brothers and the gang will—"

Before I could finish, Chris said, "Will what, throw rocks and sticks at us again?" I was trying to find something to say, but my mind kept going back to those stupid tests again. Then Chris said, "Yeah, that's what I thought," and started to stare me down. I started to think I should make a run for it.

Ethan then looked at Chris and said, "Shall we?"

"We shall," Christ confirmed and started to walk toward me.

I tried to make a run for it. But Chris caught me and yelled "Oh no, you don't!" and slammed me to the ground. They started to kick me and that's when one of them kicked me in the side of the head. Then Ethan started to slug me in the face. Then Chris said, "Let's gut this little punk," as he put the switchblade to my neck.

Then they stopped and looked up. When Chris looked up, he got nailed in the face and fell beside me. That's when I noticed that it was Dan who slugged him in the face. Dan let Chris get up and run away so he could help me up and say, "Are you all right, little bro?" He brushed me off.

"Yeah," I said, looking down, knowing that Dad was going to start yelling at me the moment I walked through the door. I had a feeling that Dan knew that too.

Dan cocked his head to the side and said, "I'll make sure he won't yell at you, Mike," smiling at me.

Then I heard Matt yell, "That's right. Don't mess with my little brother! I love him, you, you, you little Mustang drivers!" He picked up a big branch and threw it at them while they got in the car. I was surprised when it hit one of them, and they fell to the ground, but then he hopped in the car and backed up and drove off as fast as they could. Dan, the gang, and I started to laugh at him. He then turned around and said, "What are you guys laughing at? Why is that funny? I meant it, you know."

"Yeah, I know, Matt," I said, as Matt walked over to me with a big smile on his face.

"Oh, I know you know. I just want to know why you're laughing."

I shook my head and said, "Oh, Matt, Matt, Matt," starting to crack up.

Then he said, "Oh Mike, Mike, Mike, you need to learn how to do karate or something."

I gave him a weird look that meant, *Are you kidding me?* "Yeah, right," I muttered as we started to walk to the house.

When I stepped inside, Dad looked up from his newspaper then looked back down with no concern on his face. But he looked back up with an angry look on his face and took off his glasses and glared at me for a few seconds as he stood up and said, "What happened to you? Why didn't you ride the bus home like you're supposed to do?"

"I was having trouble getting my stuff in my bag and—"

But then Dan interrupted me to say "Then he got jumped by Chris and his little friends, Dad" while walking toward Dad. "And this time they got to mug him before we could get to him, so give him a break, will ya."

Dad looked back at me and said, "Is that what happened last time?" I shook my head slowly. "Then you need to stop worrying about getting your stuff together and just get on the stinking bus. Then do it on the bus so you don't get jumped, *again*," he said in a stern voice.

"Okay." I looked up at him and nodded my head lightly.

"All right, now, take a shower while I get dinner ready for the boys and you," he said, walking into the kitchen.

"What are you making today, Mr. D?" Mark asked, following Dad into the kitchen. John, David, Alex, George, Bradley, Mark, and Clark call him that because Daniel is my dad's name too. And they don't want Dan and Dad to get confused, so they call our dad Mr. D. But he doesn't like it when Dan, Matt, and I call him that. But we can get away with calling him Old Man. Usually Dan calls him that. Matt sometimes calls him Paps, and I just call him Dad, not Old Man or Paps. Nothing special or unique. Just plain old Dad.

When I got out of the shower, everyone was eating and watching the football game.

"You better hurry up and get dressed so you don't miss the game, Mike," Dan said, sitting on the couch.

"Don't worry. I am," I said, running to my bedroom.

After I got dressed, I grabbed my food, which was chicken and dumplings and delicious, by the way. Then I sat in the middle of Dan and Dad. Dad was on the right side, and Dan was on the left side of the couch. We were all rooting for the Seattle Seahawks except Bradley. He loves the Patriots, and I mean *loves* the Patriots. His whole room is all Patriots. We were wearing our Seahawk T-shirts or tank tops with plain jackets over them and baseball caps on backward or frontward, except Bradley. He was wearing his Patriots cape and T-shirt with a flannel.

When the game ended and the Seahawks won, John, David, Mark, Clark, Bradley, George, and Alex left. But Bradley was as mad at the Patriots as a hornet would be mad at a kid for bothering its nest. Dad told him sorry that his team lost. Bradley said it was all right, but we knew he wasn't happy. You could tell by the sound of his voice that he was madder than ever. There's just nothing like your favorite football team losing a game.

After we said goodbye to them, Dad started to tease Dan about not having a girlfriend yet. But Dan just said, "I work too much and too hard, which means, Dad, I'm too busy to have a girlfriend." As he cleaned the dishes, he added, "And that means I won't have time for her."

"Busy or not, they'll be excited to see you when you get home," Dad said, leaning against the counter while folding his arms.

"Well..." Dan said, not knowing what to say next.

"Well, you better find the perfect girl or I will, and I mean it too, and you know that, Danny," Dad said as he pointed at Dan and started to walk off.

Dan stopped Dad in his tracks when he said, "Why should I find the perfect girl for me, old man?" He started to fold his arms and give Dad the fake serious look.

Dad turned around and said, "Well...because I want grandkids and for you to be happy."

There was this silent laughter in the house. Then Dan said, "All right, I'll try to find one. But if I don't, you find a girl for me, deal?" He put his hand out so Dad could shake on it, and Dad said "Deal," and they shook hands.

CHAPTER 2

When I woke up the next morning, I realized it was Saturday, and my brothers, John, David, Mark, Alex, Clark, and I were going to play football at the park. Maybe George and Bradley will come too if they get done with their chores. Me, Matt, and Dan jumped in the truck and drove to the park. When we got there, John, David, Mark, Alex, and Clark were there waiting for us. But they were turned around, looking at something or someone else.

So Dan parked the truck, jumped out, and said, "What are you knuckleheads looking at, boy?" While he was talking, he put Alex's head in his armpit and rubbed his fist into Alex's head. Then David said with that bad boy look in his eyes, "Watching this new girl in town who is by the fountain reading a book."

Dan glared at them. "Why are you guys watching a girl? That's weird." As if he never looked at random girls before.

"Because she's pretty," Alex said, trying to get out of Dan's arm.

"No, she's beautiful," John said, shaking his head.

Then David said, "No, no, no, she's gorgeous," throwing his arms in the air with a big smile on his face.

"*Yeah!*" they all shouted together.

"Wait, where is she again?" Matt asked, trying to find her.

"What does she look like?" I asked, trying to find her too.

Alex was still struggling to get out of Dan's armpit when he said from behind us, "Tell your big brother to let go of me. Then we'll tell you what she looks like."

"Okay, killjoy," Dan said, letting go of him.

"Well, she has long curly hair that is gold-blond ombre, and she's wearing a white dress with a jean jacket," John said, putting his hands in his front pockets, biting his lip.

Then Matt said, "Oh, I see her. She is gorgeous. Man, I bet all the guys wish she was under their arm." He turned and looked at Dan. "Right, Daniel?" he said, lifting one eyebrow. Dan turned and looked down at him. Matt began to give him a crooked smile.

"Yep," Dan quipped. "Now let's play some football," he said, walking toward the field that we usually played football on. It seemed like he was trying to forget about the girl by the fountain. We looked at each other, wondering the same thing. What was going on in that manly mind of his? Matt ran alongside our big brother.

"Do you like her, Dan?" he asked, with a kiddish smirk. Dan didn't say anything but just glanced at him and kept walking until Matt stepped in front of him and said, "Well, do you?"

Dan was silent for a moment, then with a careless look he said, "No, why made you think that, little brother?" Dan started to walk away, but Matt stayed on his toes. "Well, you seem to be trying to hide something from us," Matt said, biting his lip. Usually when he does this, he's curious or waiting to see what the other person has to say. "You weren't acting like you were trying to hide something until you saw her pretty face, you know?"

Dan seemed to be getting mad and turned around to say, "Listen, I told you once already, I didn't like her. I just want to play some stinking, damn football…" Taking a quick pause, he spat out, "I don't like her, okay."

"Okay," Matt said back, as he flung his hands in the air. Dan turned around and started to walk away again, when Matt said with a big grin, "But you still like her. You're just lying about it."

"Oh, come on, little bro, give me a break!"

"You come on and tell me the truth, big bro," Matt said sassily, until Dan walked toward him, and he started to run backward. "Sorry, sorry, sorry," he sputtered as he sprinted behind David.

David looked at him and said, "How am I going to save you?"

"You can be my shield, man."

"Well, I'm probably going to be a waste of a shield in the end of this." David turned to look back at Dan, who was marching toward them.

"Good."

"What?" David shouted, turning around to look at Matt. But Matt just shrugged at David's concern for being his shield. Once Dan got to them, Matt tried to run for it, but Dan grabbed and put him over his shoulder.

"Hey, put me down!" Matt yelled as he kicked his feet.

"No, you turd bird."

"Fine, then I'll just fart in your face."

"You do and I'll..." He paused and sniffed. "Oh, Matt, you stink!" he said as he flipped Matt over his shoulder. Matt's farts were silent, but they sure were deadly. We all burst out laughing, besides Dan who was covering his nose, freaking out at Matt. "I mean goodness, little brother. It's almost as bad as a skunk spray, PU."

We were all laughing 'til Alex pointed out, "Sh-she's laughing at us," with a blank look on his face. We all looked to see if it was true. Even Dan looked to see. And there she was, laughing her heart out till she saw us looking at her and looked back down at her book, still smiling.

"I think we might've scared her off," Clark said, frowning.

Then out of nowhere, Matt yelled, "Did we scare you ma'am?" cupping his hands around his mouth.

John pushed him and said, "What's wrong with you?"

Matt looked at him with a big smirk and said, "Everything," in the most serious way possible. John stopped looking at him and looked at Dan, who was spacing out at the gorgeous girl by the fountain as if hypnotized by her beauty.

John smiled at him and said, "You all right there, Dan?" Dan nodded as he kept staring at that long blond curly-haired girl sitting by the fountain. "Are you sure? You seem to be falling in love," John said, sounding calm so Dan wouldn't freak out. As John spoke to Dan, I noticed that the girl by the fountain was locking eyes with him. Her grin seemed to have a bit of a shyness to it. Which made her look sweet, like an overripe peach.

Dan took in a deep breath as he said, "No, no, I'm fine, really," as he tried to look at us, but she seemed to force his eyes back on hers.

Matt smiled and said, "All right, then let's play some football!" He ran to go push Dan, but instead of Dan falling over, Matt bounced back.

This got Dan's attention, and he smiled, "Did you really think you could knock me down?"

"No, I just forgot that you're the man made out of steel," Matt said, starting to moan. Dan and John were on mine and Alex's team because they were the strongest and the oldest out of the group. Alex and I were younger and also a little bit weaker than the rest. So we get to be on their team since they were stronger than the rest of us.

"Hick!" Dan yelled. Then Alex passed it to him. Then he passed it to me, and John made sure that Matt and David didn't catch me and doggie pile on top of me. Then, if our plan works and no one catches me, I can make it to the end of the field to get a touchdown for our team. Then we do it all over again or switch it up. The reason I'm the runner is that I'm the fastest. But Dan is the best player, so he can be anything. Same with John. Dan and John were the best players on their high school teams. They could play any part of the field. Quarterback, defense, offense, and beyond. It didn't really seem to matter what part of the team they were. They could play it.

When George and Bradley saw us and asked Dan if they could play with us, Dan just said, "Of course you can, one of you go on Matt's team and the other on mine." He pointed at Matt and then him. Like I said before, they have been friends for as long as I can remember. So of course Bradley is going on Matt's team.

George ran over to me and Alex and asked, "Have you seen that new girl?"

"Yep," Alex and I said together. He put his arms on our shoulders.

"She's gorgeous, huh," he said all wide-eyed with a big smile on his face. That was when Alex started to get wide-eyed too.

"Oh, yeah, she is," he said, agreeing with George.

George took his arms off us and said, still wide-eyed, "She's the most gorgeous girl I've ever seen." I started to take off my sweatshirt.

"You know, we should go over there after this and see what she's like," I said. But I really just wanted to see if she was perfect for Dan.

"We should," George said, bobbing his head up and down. We started to play football again, and a lot of people started to watch us. Even that long blond curly-haired girl with the white dress and jean jacket, who was sitting by the fountain still, taking glances of her book with a string attached to it for a bookmark.

"Ready, set, hike!" Matt shouted. It was 3 to 2, with our team ahead. We had only been there since eight o'clock, and it had only been twenty minutes already. Everyone was running into each other. Until we saw Bradley run in the middle of us and we stopped. You could hear him say, "You'll never catch me, you imbeciles," as he ran to the end of the field. Then somehow Dan, John, Alex, George, and I got out of all the chaos and went after him. Then Matt's team went after us. You could hear Matt yell, as he put his thumb in the air, "Go, Bradley, go! Get us a touchdown so we can beat them and so our team will be the better than my brothers', okay!" Bradley started to run backward.

"*Okay!*" he said, putting his thumb in the air. Then turned back around. Me, Alex, and George couldn't help but laugh at their small plan. That was when I noticed we were falling behind, but we caught up real quick. When I saw Dan tackle Bradley, I tried to stop, but I fell on both of them. Then Alex and George fell on me. Then John, Matt, David, Mark, and Clark fell on all of us.

"Get off, you guys," Dan said, trying to get up.

"Yeah, get off, you fat butts," Bradley said as he was trying to wiggle his way out from under us.

"We can't, Matt, and all of them won't get off us," George said with his head being pushed on to his brother's back.

"Then push them off!" Bradley yelled, starting to get mad at us.

"We can't, they're too fat," Alex said, trying to push them off him.

Then I yelled, "Can you guys please get off us!" I was looking at them. But something was up, literally. They stopped pushing each other and were looking up at something or someone. "Are you guys listening...to...me?" I said slowly when I heard a giggle behind me. When I turned my head around to see who giggled, I saw two black-and-white sneakers attached to two long, skinny legs that were tan from the bright sun. As I followed them up to the person they were attached to, I started to notice that they were wearing the same clothes as that long blonde curly-haired girl. That's when it hit me: it was her. She had the most beautiful big eyes I'd ever seen in my life. They were a light baby blue. Which made me think of a summer day at the beach. But my vision was slowly ruined by someone getting warm, then really hot, and then really sweaty under me.

When I looked down, I saw that it was Dan who was getting hot and sweaty. I couldn't help but chuckle at him. Only because I knew now that he really liked her. "Holy moly, Dan, you're getting really toasty," Bradley said, beginning to laugh.

"Are you okay, Dan?" Alex asked as he put his hand on Dan's back.

"Yeah, Dan, you're getting really hot and sweaty, are you all right, big brother?" I asked, patting him on his back.

"I-I'm fine, I'm just hot and sweaty from playing football, okay," Dan said awkwardly.

"Oh, I think it might be something else," said Clark, winking at Dan.

"Oh, yeah, like what?" Dan said, looking straight through him.

"Well, maybe that pretty little young lady in front of us is wrapped around your finger, Danny," Mark said, pointing at the long blond curly-haired girl. Then everyone looked at Dan and smiled.

"Ohh, Dan, do you like her?" Matt asked with a big grin. Dan then yelled, "*What, no!*" as his face got bright red. "It's just from playing football, that's all." That was when everyone burst out laughing and jumped off him.

"Dan likes the new girl, Dan likes the new girl!" we all shouted as we started to dance around him. And the crowd of people started laughing at us.

Dan stood up and brushed himself off, and before we all started to jump on him, I noticed he looked like a big gorilla right next to her, and she was like a little china doll. He was big and buff, and she was small and skinny. Not stick skinny, she had just the right amount of curves on her. But she was sure small. I guess she noticed how small she was compared to Dan when she moved her lips, as if to say, "Oh my lord!" Then she started to bite her lip.

After we jumped on him, Dan said, "Stop it, you amateurs, you're acting like little teenage girls."

We stopped, and Matt walked up to the girl and reached out with his hand like he had a microphone in it and asked, "What's your name, pretty little lady?" giving her that chairman smile of his.

She just shook her head and giggled and said, "Jessie, Jessie Smith," shooting a crooked little smile back at him. Matt paused for a moment as he scanned her in the same position, and she looked up and down at herself then gave him a weird look. He stood up straight and said okay and turned to Dan and whispered, "Now I know why you like her so much, Dan," winking at him.

Dan just gave him an angry look and said, "All right, goofball, let's finish the game," as he grabbed Matt by the back of his shirt. I noticed Jessie winked back at Matt, and Matt grinned as she said, "So that's it, you're just going to grab your brother, I'm guessing, and leave without telling me your name. Well, actually, I know your name, but you're not going to tell me sorry or if you're okay. You're just going to walk off." She folded her arms and shot Dan a crooked little smile. At first Dan was trying to be Mr. Tough Guy. But once he saw that smile, he had to smile back at her, knowing he couldn't just walk away from her. We sat there in silence for a few seconds. Then she said, "Well, I'm waiting." She was still folding her arms but started to get a sexy look on her face.

"Well, Ms. Bossy," Dan said boldly, "my name is Daniel, and these are my brothers, Matthew and Michael." Dan pointed at Matt then me.

Then Matt added, "Or you can call us Dan, Matt, and Mike," smiling at Dan.

Then she pointed to the boys who were behind us. "And who are you friends back there?"

I said, "This is Alex, Georg, David, John, Bradley, Mark, and Clark. Which Mark and Clark are twin brothers, as you can see. And so are George and Bradley. Except they're not twins." I walked by them one at a time and touched them, making sure she knew which one was which.

Then she repeated every one of them. "So you're Alex, Georg, David, John, Bradley, Mark, and Clark. Which Mark and Clark are twin brothers, as I can see. So are George and Bradley. Except they're not twins. Got it," she said as she winked and snapped her fingers at me.

It was silent again besides kids yelling and screaming. "Well, we better finish our game before I got to go to work," Dan said, trying to sneak off.

Jessie folded her arms and said, "Oh, no, you're not getting off that easy, mister." She grabbed hold of the back of his shirt and turned him around and slapped her hands on his shoulders. Dan's face got red, but it wasn't just him. Jessie's cheeks started to get a little red too. "Man, you're really strong," she said, realizing how strong he was once she put her hands on his broad shoulders.

"Yeah, it kind of runs in the family," Dan said slowly as he began to slouch down till he was face-to-face with Jessie. We started to smile at them. We knew what was going on in the air. Jessie then slid her hands off Dan's shoulders while saying, "I'm so sorry, I—"

That was when Dan blurted, "No, i-it's fine. I don't mind…at all." A short moment passed before Dan said, "So you can put your hands back…if you want."

Jessie laughed and said, "I'm good, thanks." That was when it got silent between the two of them, and they were just four inches away from kissing. But the silence ended once David asked, putting his hand to his chin, "How old are you?"

"David, that's rude to ask someone," Alex said, giving him a nasty look.

"Oh, it's fine, Alex, but how old do you think I am?" Jessie asked, trying to look at us, while Dan couldn't take his eyes off her for even a second. "Well, hell, I don't know." He shrugged. "You look eighteen, to be honest, but act twenty, so somewhere around there," he said, moving his hand in a circular motion.

"Well, I'm twenty-one years old, so you were pretty close," Jessie said, spacing out back into Dan's eyes.

"Really, Dan's that age too," Matt said, looking confused but with a smile.

"Well, that's nice, but, um, my brothers won't let me have a boyfriend, if that's what you were going for," she said, giving Matt an "I'm sorry" look. When she said that, Dan's happiness quickly faded.

"That's exactly what we were going for," Matt said, sounding like he didn't hear what she said to him.

"Well, I got to go home and take care of my dog then get done working on decorating the house. But it was nice meeting you guys," she said, starting to walk away.

But then something came over Dan. He grabbed her hand and asked, "Will we see you again?" as if worried that he would never see her beautiful face again.

She smiled and turned around to say, "I come here every morning at seven fifty to walk my dog or read a book." He smiled at the fact of her being here every morning.

"Okay, so I'll see you? I mean, we will see," he said, letting go of her hand.

She smiled once more and said, "Maybe." We watched her leave.

"Ooooohhh, Dan!" we said together.

Dan turned around and said, "Shut up and let's finish that game." Dan started to walk to the field, and we all followed him to continue our game.

Dan took Matt and me home and went off to work after the game. It ended at 13 to 10, with Dan's team ahead. After he dropped us off, Matt and I raced to the front door to tell Dad all about this girl that Matt and I thought was perfect for Dan. When we did, Dad just smiled and said, "Well, that's good, but does he like her, and does she like him?" He looked at us worriedly.

"Well, he got hot and sweaty when he saw her and asked her if he would see her again, and she said *maybe*, and she also got red cheeked when she touched his shoulders, but not only that. When they looked in each other's eyes, it was like, like they were meant to be," Matt said, looking at Dad with a grin.

"All righty then, so you really think this girl is perfect for your big brother?" Dad asked, turning around to look at us.

"Yeah," Matt and I said at the same time.

"Okay, then let's try and get these two lovebirds together, boys."

CHAPTER 3

It was 1:35 p.m. when I got finished with my lunch and decided to call Alex's house and ask if he would go on a walk with me.

"Why, are you scared that Chris and his friends might jump you again?" Alex said.

"That and how we're going to get Dan and Jessie together," I said, joyful.

"All right, let's get these two together," he said in an excited voice.

"Okay, let's meet in the park," I said as I laughed.

When we met at the park, no one was there. So Alex and I started to play on the playground and began to act like we were dumb little rich kids. "Look at me, I'm a little stupid rich kid going to jump off these little stupid monkey bars and break my little ankle," Alex said, standing on the monkey bars.

"Be careful, Alex, you might break your crown jewels," I said worriedly. I jinxed it. He slipped, fell, and then hit his crown jewels on the metal monkey bars.

He then slipped off to the ground, with his hands in between his legs, and said, "Why did you say that, Mike?"

"I'm sorry, I didn't mean to jinx you, but you did it to yourself. I warned you that it wasn't a good idea," I said as I patted him.

"Don't touch me, you, you jackass," he said as he slapped my hand, but then he started to cry.

"I didn't mean to jinx you, you know that, right. I just was trying to warn you that it might happen," I said, starting to get mad at myself for breaking my friend's crown jewels.

"I know you didn't mean to," he said, getting up.

"Then why are you blaming me?" I asked, starting to get angrier.

"I'm sorry, it just hurts, you know," he said, bending down like he was going to throw up.

"It's fine," I said, shrugging. "And no, I don't know that it hurts, because I don't do stupid things like you do." I patted him on the back again.

"Let's just go and forget this even happened, okay," he said, sitting up.

"Good idea," I said as we started to walk into town.

Then Alex asked me, "Why does it hurt so much, Mike?"

I just looked at him and said, "I don't know, Alex, I just don't know."

When we got in town, Alex and I stopped at Farrell's Ice Cream Parlor, which was the closest ice cream place to the park. Our moms used to take us there all the time, till we got old enough to walk on our own.

"So how are we going to get Dan and Jessie together?" Alex asked as he took big licks of his ice cream, which was rocky road ice cream, his favorite. My favorite ice cream was swirl with hot fudge on it.

"I think we should get Dan's number first and give it to her and say it was ours," I said, licking my ice cream.

"Sounds good. But …" Alex said, starting to stop licking his ice cream.

"But what?" I said, starting to stop licking my ice cream too.

"It's just, I don't want to lie to her," he said, starting to lick his ice cream again.

"Why?" I asked, thinking the plan over in my head, trying to think of what was such a bad lie.

"I don't know. It just feels wrong to lie to a girl, you know," he said, shrugging. "Especially one as nice as Jessie Smith."

"I guess," I said, sitting there, looking at my ice cream, trying to see where I should lick it next.

"Any other ideas?" he asked, starting to look at his ice cream too.

"Not really," I said, finding a good spot to lick. "Yeah, I guess we're just going to have to deal with plan A, huh, Mike," Alex said, beginning to lick his ice cream some more.

"I guess so, buddy, or we can just give her Dan's number and say that it's his," I said, trying to finish my ice cream before he does. We sat there for a moment till Alex asked, "Are you trying to race me, Mike?" raising one eyebrow.

"Um, no," I said, pausing after every lick as a smile appeared on my face.

"Yes, you are, you little liar."

"Okay, okay, I am," I said, rolling my eyes.

"All right, let's see who can finish their ice cream first," Alex said, pulling his ice cream closer to him.

"On the count of three," I said, getting ready to chow down my cone.

"One, two, *three*!" we said. And the race was on. Alex and I started to chow down our cones as fast as we could. But it seemed to me that we were going to get done at the same time. People started to stare at us as if we were freaks, but we didn't care. We were boys. In the end, Alex won. We started to walk to Dan's work. Which was a shop in town where you could go and get your car or motorcycle fixed. Dan's a mechanic who fixes both cars and motorcycles. When we got there, a woman was in the front counter, which was Ms. Sans, who was the ugliest and meanest woman I've ever met. She's fat and has big wrinkles on her face with old lady glasses sitting on the edge of her nose. She also has a huge mole on her right cheek.

Me and Alex knew she didn't like us too much. Probably because we once scared the devil out of her when we went in someone's car and it started to move. To be honest with you, I don't know what the big deal was. We were just stupid little preteens trying to learn how to drive a car so we could pass our driver's test. When we asked her if we could see Dan, she gave us a real nasty look and said, "No, you can't, he's too busy to see you two—"

Then Dan interrupted her and said, "It's okay, Ms. Sans, I'm not busy anymore." He walked toward us, cleaning his hands off with a red rag with oil stains on it.

"Okay, Dan, whatever you say, but make sure they don't touch anything, okay. I don't want you to lose your job because of these two—"

Dan interrupted her again and said, "I know, Ms. Sans, I'll keep my eye on these two knuckleheads, don't worry."

"All right, Dan, I trust you!" Ms. Sans said as we walked away.

"Okay, you two heard her. Don't touch anything or I'll lose my job, understood," Dan said, walking backward and pointing at us.

"Yep, we understand, Dan," Alex said as he snapped his fingers and pointed at Dan.

"Good, now tell me why are you two here at my work," he said, grabbing a wrench out of the toolbox and started to work on a car.

"Well, we…came…here…to…to…Why did we come here again?" Alex asked, squinting at me.

"We came here to see if you're busy tomorrow," I said.

"Why?" he said, looking suspicious.

"Uhh, so we can play football at the park." I paused when he turned around and started to look right through my plan. "Without you having to leave it in an hour or so," I said, slowly trying to regress our plan.

"Oh really," Dan said, turning to look in the toolbox again.

"Really!" Alex said, trying to look serious.

"Or do you want to just tease me and say that I like the new girl over and over again," he said, smiling at us.

"No!" Me and Alex yelled.

"No, no, no, Dan, we wouldn't do that," I said, shaking my hands back and forth.

"Yes, you would. You were doing it earlier today. So don't lie to me," Dan said playfully.

"We're not going to tease you, Dan. We are just going to get you with Jessie, that's all," Alex said with a worried sound to his voice. Dan looked at us shyly.

"Is that really all?" Dan said slowly, looking straight through us again as he stood up once he found the tool he was looking for.

"Yeah, Dan, that's really all," I said, shrugging.

"I don't know, boys. I'm a little rusty. Not only that, but I work too hard and—"

Before he finished, I said, "Didn't you ever listen to what Mom told you before you moved out, Daniel?" The moment he looked at me, I knew I got him.

"Okay, fine, this Sunday, so tomorrow," he said, pointing at us with the screwdriver.

"Okay, sounds good," Alex said, turning around to leave.

"Oh, and can we have your number too?" I said. holding out my hand.

And I heard Dan whisper "Oh, what are you getting yourself into, Daniel?" as he picked up a pen and wrote down his number.

"Thanks, Dan. Now you might not be lonely anymore," I said, grabbing the piece of paper.

He glared at me when I said that, so I said sorry to him.

"It's okay, we'll meet at the park at 8:00 a.m., okay," he said, giving us the piece of paper with his number on it.

"Okay," I said as we walked away.

After that, me and Alex were walking to my house when we went past the park and saw Jessie with a German shepherd, reading that book again all alone by the fontina. "Should we go over there?" Alex asked as his eyes begged me to say yes.

"Well, yeah, we kind of need to so we can give her Dan's number," I said, holding up the piece of paper. As we were walking over there, the dog saw us and trotted over to us.

"Don't worry, he's friendly," Jessie said, taking her eyes off her book then looking back.

"He looks friendly," Alex said, petting her dog.

"What's his name?" I asked as I was petting him.

"Romeo," she said as she stood up.

"He looks like a Romeo to me. Good name," Alex said, sitting back up.

"Yep, he's my good boy, huh, Romeo," she said, and Romeo barked back at her, and she giggled.

Then Alex nudged me and said, "Well, give her his number and ask her for hers, Mike."

I pulled out Dan's number and said, "Here's Dan's number. He wanted us to give it to you." I held it out for her to take it. She hesitated for a moment then said with a worried stiff expression, "Oh no, I can't. My brothers, they will figure out that I have his number."

"If we don't let them know? Besides, it's your choice," I said, still holding it out for her to take it.

"I guess so, but ..." she said, clutching tightly to her book.

"But what? There's nothing to be afraid of, and you don't have to show him to your brothers right away. I say wait three or four weeks to show him so then you at least know a lot about him and what he's like," Alex said, taking the piece of paper out of my hand and trying to make her take it.

"Yeah, I guess I could do that, I mean, Dan is very sweet as far as I know," she said with a big smile. "Big but sweet," she said as her cheeks started to blush.

Then I yelled, pointing at her, "Exactly, you get him!"

"Well, does he get me?" she said, holding tighter to her book.

"Well, I don't know, he never said anything. But he likes you, I can tell, he's my big brother, I know him," I said, keeping my vocals low.

"But you don't know me, now do you," she said, losing her grip on her book.

"Yeah, but I know you good enough to know you're perfect for my brother and that you like him," I said, throwing my arms in the air.

"And we'll get to know you more when you're with Mike's big brother," Alex added.

"I guess so, but you know you can't just make two people who barely know each other like each other, right?" she said, losing her temper a bit.

"First off, yes, we can. Second, I'm not trying to, I just want you two to open up to each other because I know you guys really do like each other. So don't lie to me, little missy," I said, unfolding my arms.

She smiled at me. "I do really like your brother," she said. "It's just my brothers that worries me." She sighed as her smile started to fade away.

"So it's your brothers that are holding you back from falling in love with Dan?" Alex asked.

I started to talk to Alex, "If so, my brother won't care if they beat him up if he really likes her. He'll just fight with words but not punch them or anything."

I guess she heard me talking to Alex and said, "Really," starting to smile again.

"Really," Alex and I said at the same time.

She bit her lip and, smiling even more, said, "Okay, I'll give it a shot."

"Good, now can you meet us tomorrow at 8:00 a.m. here?" I said as I pointed at the ground.

"Yeah, I'm going to be coming here at 7:55 a.m. anyways because it's part of my morning routine," she said with a smile.

"All right, see you tomorrow, Jessie," Alex said, and we started to leave.

Then she asked, "Do you want me to take you home?"

We turned back around, and I said, "Sure."

"Okay, hop in my little cute red Chevy Impala and show me the way to your house," she said, swinging her keys around. We hopped in her little red Chevy Impala, even her dog, and drove off to my house.

When we got there, we said thanks to Jessie for giving us a ride in her cute little red Chevy impala then ran inside. When we got in there, my dad was looking out the window. He looked at us with a confused-looking face and asked, "Who was that?"

"That's the girl me and Matt told you about, Dad," I said as Alex and I walked into the kitchen, looking for something to eat.

"Oh really," Dad said, turning away from the window.

"Really, Mr. D," Alex said, looking through the cupboard.

"Hey, I'll make dinner in a minute, so stop looking through the cupboards, boys!" Dad said, walking into the kitchen to shoo us out. Alex and I got out of the kitchen so Dad could make us dinner and went to my bedroom.

"Man, your brother is sure lucky, isn't he," Alex said, hopping on my bed.

"Yeah, he sure is," I said, looking for a pair of pajama pants.

"I wonder if they'll make it," Alex said as he lay down on my bed. "Do you think they'll make it?"

"They probably will," I said, still trying to find those stupid pajama pants.

"Why do you think that?" he asked, sitting up on my bed.

"Well, I don't know. I just got a feeling that Jessie's brothers will lighten up with them being together once they see how much they love each other," I said once I finally found my pajama pants.

"Yeah, probably," Alex said, laying back down.

I was in the shower when I heard Alex bang on the door and say, "I need to go to the bathroom, man, hurry up, like now." I could also hear him potty dancing on other side of the door.

"Okay, hold on," I said, trying to scrub all the soap out of my hair.

"I've been holding on too long," he said, still jumping.

"Then go outside, Alex. You're a big boy now, aren't ya?" Matt said as he walked by him.

"No, I don't want anyone to see me," Alex said, starting to stop potty dancing.

I hopped out of the shower, wrapped a towel around my waist, grabbed my clothes, and opened the door and said, "All yours, Alex."

"Thank you for hurrying, Mike," Alex said, going past me.

"No problem," I said as I shut the door. I went in my bed and got dressed in my clean pajamas and went in the living room. Dan, Matt, John, Mark, Clark, David, Bradley, George, and Alex were all lined up for dinner in that exact order. "Hey, what are we having, Dad?" I asked as I got in line. Then David said "Knuckle sandwiches" as he turned around and he put his fist up. We just laughed at him.

"It's lasagna, Mike," Dan said as he went by with his food.

After we all got our food, Dad brought up Jessie to Dan. "So I heard you like this new girl in town, huh." Dan immediately stopped eating when he heard *new girl* but grinned. "The boys told me all about her. How she likes you and how you like her. That's good, Dan," Dad said as Dan's smile grew to a big grin while he slowly turned to look at Matt and me. Then he said "Oh yeah" and went back to eating.

"So are you going to see her again, Dan?" Dad asked, as Dan went to put his plate in the sink.

"He better go," Alex said, taking his eyes off the television.

"Yeah, Daniel, you better go," Dad said, smiling even more, as Dan came back to the couch to sit back down.

"Don't worry, I will. It's just ..." Dan sighed, half smiling.

"Oh, I see you're shy about talking about your feelings for her, huh," Dad said, getting up to put his plate away. Dan just looked down and chuckled as he muttered, "No, I just...don't...really want..." Dan paused to take in a deep breath to relax himself then said, "For her to see ..."

That was when Dad blurted from the kitchen, "To see what? Your junk?" The room quickly fluted with laughter as Dan looked at Dad with an unexpected look.

After a moment passed, Dan said, "No, Dad, that's not why." He said it in a bit of an angry and depressed way. More of a depressed way, though. Usually this is his sign of getting someone to be a little bit more serious in the conversation. Dad of course knew this, so he quit joking and sat down next to Dan to say, "All right, what is it?" And the room got quiet.

"I don't want her to see the beast in me," Dan said with an ill expression.

Dad put his hand on Dan's shoulder with a light smile and said, "Oh, Dan, a woman that truly loves you isn't going to battle your demons but help you overcome them, you understand?" Dan nodded his head in awareness. "Okay, now one other thing," Dad said as he took his hand off Dan's shoulder and put one finger in the air. "Do not, and I mean do not be hiding things from a woman," he said as he walked into the kitchen.

"Why, Dad?"

"Well, because if you keep your feelings to yourself, she's just going to think you're cheating on her or don't love her or you're scared, and that scares them," Dad said as Dan stood up.

"Why would they think that?" Dan questioned with confusion.

"Because it makes them think you're not sure about them or what you want, and a lot of women don't like a man who isn't sure about what they want, so remember that. And stop asking questions or else," Dad said, going into the kitchen to put his plate in the sink, 'till Dan asked with a smirk across his face, "Or else what, old man?"

"Or I'm going to go over there and beat the devil out of you, little man," Dad said, pointing a finger at him with a serious look.

"Oh, Dad, I think you're getting old, because he's a big, big man, not little man," Matt said, looking at Dad with his charming smile.

"Yeah, he's a big muscle man," Bradley said with a smolder, flexing his arms in the air.

"You're right, what am I talking about, boys?" Dad said as he shrugged.

"I don't know, Mr. D, I don't know."

"See you tomorrow at 8:00 a.m., Dan," I said, hanging outside the door, waving at Dan. He turned around and waved back at me. I hate seeing Dan leave the house. The only reason is that Dad usually starts a fight with me. That's usually about my grades or I came home really late at night. Although, Dan's just across the street, so I can just walk over there if Dad is being too rough on me.

"Hey, Mike!" Dad yelled in the kitchen.

"Yeah, Dad," I said as I slowly closed the door.

"Is he really going to see this beautiful girl you been telling me about?" he asked as I walked into the kitchen. "He better, 'cause I know she is going to be there for sure," I said, leaning against the entrance of the kitchen.

"And what if he doesn't?" Dad said, wiping his hands off with a wash rag.

"I'll tell him he's just an unloving young man who will be lonely the rest of his life if he doesn't meet this girl," I said, about to walk out of the kitchen.

Then Dad said, bobbing his head up and down, "That will probably tick him off. Don't you think?"

"Why do you say that?" I asked, turning back around to look at him.

"Well, you know Dan, he's sensitive when it comes to the way he feels about a girl," Dad said, walking out of the kitchen.

"Do you think he'll actually go, Dad?" I said, following Dad into the living room.

"I don't know, that's why I asked you, but I do know that it's way past your bedtime, little man, and now that's why I'm going to tell you to get your butt to bed," Dad said, turning to look at me.

"But it's—"

Before I could finish, Dad said, sounding all serious, "Oh no, no buts, straight to bed for you, man."

"Yeah, go to bed, Mike," Matt said, peeking out from the shadows.

"Okay, okay, fine, I'll go to bed," I said, putting my hands in the air.

"Good night, Mike," Dad said as he started to fold our clothes.

"Good night, Dad," Matt and I said as we raced to our bedrooms. When Dan lived here, we had to sleep in the same bed. And Matt would talk and talk all night. So I was happy that Dan left. But also sad too because the house was going to have one person emptier. But it turned out that he will always come back home to us because a house that once was home will always be home.

That night I sat in my room, thinking about tomorrow. Were Jessie and Dan going to like each other even more than they already did? Was Dan going to be shy or was Jessie? I was asking myself a whole bunch of questions. Wondering what it would be like to fall in love and hold a girl as beautiful as Jessie Smith. But I think I'm not ready for girls yet. Besides, I like books and movies better.

CHAPTER 4

The next morning I woke up throwing the covers off me, rushing to get dressed. Because today was the day where love was in the air. Oh, and the sweet smell of breakfast too. When I walked into the living room, Dad was in the kitchen, cooking eggs and bacon. He looked at me and said, "Well, good morning, sleepyhead. You want some eggs and bacon?"

"Sure, thanks," I said, walking into the kitchen and grabbing a plate.

"Why are you not at work yet?" I asked as I grabbed some eggs.

"They called and told me that everyone will be there at 11:00 a.m. today," he said as he flipped the eggs and bacon over.

"Really, why?" I asked, remembering how one time some delinquent kids screwed up the machinery and teepeed the place, so Dad wasn't going to be able to go to work until 5:30 p.m.

"I don't know, they never told me why," Dad said, shrugging and putting the eggs on my plate. "Oh, and your grades for testing came in the mail today," he said as he grabbed the piece of paper and showed it out in front of me. Once I grabbed it, a puny fear came over me. I knew if it wasn't good or amused my dad that he would shame me and forbid me to go anywhere. Well, to be technical, he would probably make me go someplace that I don't want to go or do work. But I unfolded the piece of paper anyway, and to my surprise, it wasn't that bad, not at all.

The piece of paper said, "*We are proud of your son for being an excellent and amazing student of Richland High School. Your son Michael Herman is at eleventh grade level and has improved since the first few months of being here. His grades in the beginning of the year after taking the tests were C-, D-, A, F, and a B- in sciences, history, ELA, math, and writing class lab. Now they're an A, B+, A, B-, and an A- in sciences, history, ELA, math, and writing class lab. We are thankful to have your son at Richland High School..."*

The rest of it just talked about the teachers and how they thought of me and all that.

"Congratulations, little man, you did it. I'm proud of you," Dad said, patting me on the back as if he was proud.

"Thanks, Dad," I said, giving him the piece of paper back.

"Yeah, thanks for the breakfast, Dad," Matt said as he walked in the kitchen, taking my plate and my eggs. I didn't do anything though. I just took another plate out because I was feeling too good this morning.

Dad gave Matt an "Are you kidding me" look and said, "We're talking about something else, Matt."

"What are you talking about then?" he asked, stuffing my breakfast in his mouth.

"How your little brother is in eleventh grade level," Dad said, putting an arm around my shoulders.

"Really good job, Mikey. You're doing better than me. I'm at tenth grade level," he said while slapping me on the back and stuffing more eggs and bacon in his mouth.

"You're a lot more intelligent than I am," he said as food flew out of his mouth. Dad looked at him with a disgusted expression and said, "Don't talk with your mouth full or else I'm going to start calling you luma boy, okay, Matthew," turning to put another two eggs on the pan. Matt looked at him, taking another big bite and said, "Okay, Paps." Then once Dad turned around and acted like he was going to slap him in the butt with the spatula, he squealed like a little girl.

After that, we hurried up and ate our breakfast and ran to Dan's house. When my hand reached out to open the door, Dan threw it open. "Wow, Mike, didn't know you were coming over here," Dan said, smiling as he walked out and shut the door behind him.

"Ready, Freddy," Matt said as we walked down the steps.

"Ready as I'll ever be," Dan said, hopping inside his truck.

"Let's get her done, hun," Matt said, sliding into the truck.

Dan looked at him and said, "I'm not your hun, you bun." Matt just laughed at him and put his seat belt on. We drove to John's house to go and pick up the gang. But there wasn't enough room inside the truck, so some of us had to go in the back of the truck.

When we got there, we saw Chris and his friends sitting by Jessie. But Jessie didn't look happy. So we all hopped out of the truck and fast walked over to them. Chris kept touching her cheeks, legs, and her hair. If you were there, you knew they were going to get their head knocked in if they didn't stop bugging and touching her, because she was going to be part of our gang and was going to be Dan's future wife, and they were going to get it. When we got closer, I could hear Dusty say "Hey, little lady, that's a pretty necklace you got there, is it your great grandmother's?" and ripped her necklace off her neck.

"Hey, give it back. That's my mom's necklace. She gave it to me before she died," she said, trying to get it back as she stood up and reached for it. Then Chris was going to pull her dress up.

Till Dan grabbed him and threw him in the fontina. Jessie's eyes got wide when that happened but began to laugh at him when he started cursing Chris out. After Dan threw Chris, we went after the rest of his friends. "Give her necklace back or we'll do more than just throw rocks and sticks at you and put you in the fontina with your little friend," said John, holding Dusty in the air with one hand. Dusty gave her necklace to him, and John dropped him on the ground. "You belong on the ground because you're *dusty*," John said, grinning. "Here's your necklace, Jessie," he said, holding it out for her to take it.

"Thanks, I thought they were going to steal it," she said as she grabbed it with her tiny soft woman hand. After, Chris ran out of the fontina, and his friends ran to his car and drove off like the devil was after them.

Dan asked her "Are you okay, Jessie?" after he got done cursing Chris out.

"Yeah, I'm all right, Dan," she said, giggling.

"What's so funny?"

"Nothing, it's just you have a big mouth for such a nice guy."

"Oh yeah, I forgot to tell you that …" Dan said, taking a deep breath in. "And, um, sorry we're a little late," Dan continued, putting a hand behind his neck.

"A little, it's eight twenty," she said, looking at her watch.

"Really?" Dan said with funny and surprised look.

"Yep," she said, taking her eyes off her watch.

"That's a nice-looking watch, by the way, where did you get it?" Mark said, pointing at her gold-colored watch.

"Thanks, my dad gave it to me. It was his when he was a young teen," she said in a sad voice.

"Is your dad dead too?" Bradley asked, tilting his head to one side. Then Dan elbowed him in the ribs and hard. "Ow, what was that for!" he yelled at Dan.

"You don't ask someone that, Bradley. Especially a girl," Dan explained angrily.

"Oh, I'm…I'm sorry, I wasn't thinking right. I'm truly sorry," Bradley said all worriedly.

"It's fine, Bradley, you didn't know," she said, looking at him with her big puppy-dog eyes.

"Oh good, I thought you were going to start crying, then Dan was going to kick my head in." He paused to look at Dan then looked black at Jessie. "But is your dad with your mom?" Bradley asked with his hands folded in front of him.

"Yeah," she said playing with her necklace. "They died when I was ten years old, so my oldest brother, Joshua, had to take care of me and my other brothers after he graduated," she said, looking like she was about to cry.

"What's the rest of your brothers' names?" Clark said, trying to talk about something good before she started crying.

"Well, there's Justin, who's the second oldest, Joseph, who's the third, and then there's Jason, who thinks I should have a boyfriend but sometimes says I shouldn't because they are a bit, let's just say, childish," she said as we started to walk into town.

"Childish?" Bradley repeated.

"That's what he said," Jessie answered back with a shrug.

"Well, not all of us are childish," Dan shyly murmured. We all looked at Dan, wondering if he was talking about himself. He snarled and said, "I didn't mean me. I'm just trying to say some are childish but not all, like me." We laughed at him because we knew he was trying to show Jessie he was a good young man.

When we got into town, we all decided to show Jessie around and went to Farrell's Ice Cream Parlor and got some ice cream. Alex and I got the same ones as yesterday. John and Dan got vanilla. Matt got double chocolate chip ice cream. Georg and David got the same as Bradley, which was strawberry, and Jessie got a milkshake. But while we went to Farrell's Ice Cream Parlor, Mark and Clark went to go get some beers for Mark then met us back here.

"I've got a question for you two," Matt said, pointing at Dan and Jessie.

"What?" they said, looking at each other.

"Are you two going to hang out more?" Matt asked, suspicious.

"Maybe," Dan and Jessie said, smiling at each other.

Then Bradley said, "Is this a bad time to ask, who's paying for the ice cream?" when he saw Mark and Clark peeking through the glass window outside. Jessie smiled gratefully and said, "Oh, I'll pay for it." She took her wallet out of her jean jacket.

"What, no, I'll pay for it," Dan said, taking out his wallet.

"It's fine, Daniel, I can pay for it. I know how, don't worry," she said brassily.

"I know you know how. It just doesn't seem polite to make a girl pay for the food on the first date, now does it," Dan said, opening his wallet.

Jessie inhaled a deep sigh. "All right, you win, but I'll do it next time, okay," she said, putting her wallet back in her jacket. Dan put $2.86 on the table. Then we stepped out to go take a walk.

"How long have you been here, Jessie?" Dan asked as the guys and I started to wrestle around behind them. Besides, David was checking out girls like the usual as we walked along the sidewalk.

"About three or four days ago, why?" Jessie said with a favorable smile. It came to me that no matter what was going on with Jessie, she seemed to smile at everything and everyone. Which was good because Dan needed to wake up with a pretty face smiling at him.

"Just wondering," Dan said, too shy to look at her. But he couldn't help but look at her pretty face, and they started to stare in each other's eyes again. 'Till John got tired of Bradley stopping in front of him, so he accidentally pushed him into Dan and Jessie.

"Wow, you guys, knock it off right now," Dan said.

"Well, tell Mr. Stop to stop stopping in front of me. Then I'll knock it off," John said even angrier.

"Knock it off, Bradley, before I knock you off your own two feet," Dan said playfully.

Jessie just giggled and said, "Oh, you boys, so unexpectedly funny, especially you, Dan."

Dan started to get a bit of red cheeks and shyly said as he put his hand on his neck, "What are you saying, you think I could be a hot comedian?" She just shook her head, giggling, and started to walk again.

"Aww, Dan, you got her wrapped around your finger, don't cha," Matt said, giving Dan a playful punch on the shoulder.

"Nah, I'm just getting to know her," Dan said, going after her.

"He's growing up so fast," Mark said, acting like he was shedding some tears.

"Yeah, his momma would be proud," John said, putting one elbow on my shoulder.

"Yeah, she would," Matt said, smiling at them as they walked farther and farther away from us. That was when Dan yelled, "Are you guys coming, or are you just going to stand there and stare at us freakishly?" He was walking backward. "Creepy guys, okay," he added.

Then we all snapped out of it and ran over to them. "So where are we going now, Dan?" George asked, jogging up to him.

"We're going to my work to get something, okay," Dan said.

"All right, Dan, sounds good," David said, patting Dan's shoulder.

"Wait...where are we going again?" Mark said, looking at all of us.

"Really," Dan said, turning around. "Really, you weren't listening to what I just got done saying like ten seconds ago?" Dan said, stopping everyone.

"Sorry, I might have had one too many beers before I left, am I right, my twin?" Mark asked Clark.

"Yep, my twin, you had one too many beers, all right," Clark said, smiling.

Like I told you guys, Mark's the bad one out of all of us. He drinks, smokes, and even went to jail twice too. The first time was because he got caught fighting with a few rich teenagers on the street while he was drunk. The second time was because he pulled a knife on some rich kid who was trying to start a fight with him, until he saw the knife, then he cried wah, wah all the way to the police station and told them that Mark was going to kill him. But we all knew that was a lie. After going to jail twice, Mark said he was never going to go back there ever again, and he hasn't. Well, at least not yet. But I shouldn't jinx it though.

The second bad one is Bradley. Although he hasn't gone to jail, he's still is as bad as Mark. But not that bad. He only drinks and smokes, and that's pretty much it. But his brother, George, doesn't. Because his parents threatened him that they would put him in a boys' home and he'll never see them or his brother or the gang ever again. At first my dad thought they were a bad influence to me and Matt, once he found out Bradley was drinking beers at our house, but when he met their parents, that changed his mind, and he said it was fine.

But the worst person we know is Blake Frederick. Now Blake is the kind of guy that you wish was just wearing a costume all the time. But those scars are real, all right. Blake is more than just mean; he looks mean too with that huge scar across his eye that he wears with pride. That was from a blade fight in New York on the west side. Someone tried to cut his eye out with a five-inch blade. But that isn't his only scar. He also has one on his left shoulder from a gun shooting that was also in New York. And also has a scar that goes to his right side of his chest to his bottom left side of his chest, which is from another blade fight in New York. After he got out of the hospital, he came to our town and made a gang. Ever since that, he's been going to jail every a month, nonstop.

For all the reason of getting into jail. Like robbing stores, stealing the rich kids' cars, or slashing their tires, or stealing their cars and dropping them off somewhere, and some things he does I can't explain.

When we first met him, it wasn't pretty. I mean, at first it wasn't that bad at all, 'till he saw Dan and started to make fun of how big he was for a sixteen-and-a-half-year-old. Which Dan was taking pretty good. Till Blake said, "Probably nothing more than a boy with beef." After he said that, we knew Dan wasn't going to let it go anymore. He pulled his arm back and knocked him straight in the jaw and Blake fell flat on the ground. That day was the day that Dan purposely hurt someone. Usually when he'd hurt someone at that age, it was in football or wrestling. The coaches said it was because he was amazingly strong and didn't know it. So I wasn't surprised that he broke Blake's jaw. None of us were by how big and muscular he was, and he still is. From picking up tires and building houses.

Yeah, not surprised at all.

Once we got to Dan's work, Ms. Sans was surprised to see a girl with Dan and said, "Now who's this pretty little lady, Danielle, is she your girlfriend?" taking Jessie's hands with a big fat grin. Then Alex whispered, "That's the first time I've ever seen her smile at someone, besides herself," and I about laughed out loud. Till Ms. Sans glared at us as if we've done something wrong.

"This is Jessie Smith Ms. Sans, and yes, she's, um…my girlfriend." Dan looked at Jessie and then back at Ms. Sans.

"Oh, am I now, Dan," Jessie said, raising one eyebrow and putting her hands on her hips.

"Well, of course you are or will be," Dan said, being funny.

Jessie just shook her head and said, "Uh-huh."

"What do you mean 'uh-huh'? I meant it, you should know that, little missy," Dan said then began biting his lip, looking straight in her angel eyes, not saying a word for the longest moment. Jessie didn't say anything either, and at that moment, I thought they might smooch. Then Dan said, "Well anyways, I'm here to get my papers for the motorcycle that came in today." He was trying to take his eyes off her, but he was hypnotized by her gorgeousness.

"Oh, go ahead, just watch your little brother and his friend. You remember what happened last time, don't you?" she said, giving Dan a serious look.

"Yeah, I remember," Dan said, looking at Alex and me with a silly smile.

"What happened?" Jessie said with curiosity written all over her face.

"I'll tell you while we get the papers," Dan said as we started to walk into the workshop.

Dan was halfway through the story when a man said, "Hey, Dan, who's this beautiful young-looking woman?"

"This is Jessie, she's—"

Then Jessie blurted, "Kind of his girlfriend. He hasn't earned the privilege to call me his girlfriend," as she smirked at Dan.

"What she said," Dan said as he pointed at Jessie.

The man just chuckled and said, "Okay, see you tomorrow, Dan."

"See ya," Dan said, waving.

After, Dan got his paper, and we all got out of there and started to walk to the park where the truck was. "Where do you live?" Dan asked.

"I live on Carol Street, why?" Jessie said, smirking at him.

"Um…well, so I can find you if you're in trouble," Dan said as we stopped by his truck.

"What? Me in trouble? Never," Jessie said sarcastically.

"Well, what about earlier today?" Dan said with a big grin.

"That was a test," Jessie said slowly.

"Oh, so all of that was just a play, huh?"

"Yep," Jessie said, trying to hold in her laughter.

"You know what I just noticed?" Mark said, looking at both of them.

"What?" Dan said, turning toward him.

"You're just a big, high and mighty man, and she's just a tiny, little dinky woman," Mark said, pointing at them one at a time.

"Yeah," Bradley said, agreeing with him.

Jessie giggled and said, "Well, I better get going. I got to go to work in, like, thirty minutes," she said as she looked at her watch.

"Yeah, okay, and I need to…um…do something with…these… motorcycle papers," Dan said, pausing, trying to figure out all the right words to say.

"Okay." She giggled.

"Bye, see you tomorrow, maybe," Dan said.

"Maybe, bye," Jessie said as she ran to her car waving at Dan.

But then I noticed she was running back. Did she forget something? Why was she coming back? Why was she running back? "Hey, Dan, she's coming back," I said gradually.

"Ohh, she want more of you, Dan," David said, being a dork. Dan turned back, facing the direction Jessie had run and was now running back. "Wh—" he began. Then went "Oph" when Jessie jumped on him to give him a hug. He laughed a little bit before saying, "Well, warn me next time. You're a lot stronger than you look. It was like a bear body slammed me." Sounding edgy. "I mean, my lord, you almost knocked me clear off my feet, little woman," Dan said, sounding exaggerated. Jessie started to crack up, and Dan just kept bringing on the jokes like a comedian on showbiz. "I'm getting old, woman. You got to be careful or my hips will crack." He paused for a moment then said one last thing, "You're hurting meh, you're hurting meh hips, woman!" He shouted like an old man.

Jessie took down her laughter to a soft giggle and said, "Oh, I'm sorry, am I a little too heavy for you, big man?" Oh my lord that huge grin on Dan's face when she said *big man*. It was the kind of grin you would see on Matt's or David's face when they see a cute girl. So that's when I really started to think they were going to kiss. Dan, however, was going to kiss Jessie, but Jessie pressed her pointer finger on his lips and said, "No," like a child. And the depressing-disappointment expression on Dan's face quickly appeared.

"Why?" he whined.

Jessie smiled at him as she unwrapped her legs from his hips and whispered loudly, "Because I don't know you well enough, that's why, my darling Daniel." Dan's eyes were now wide, which made him look funny. Especially the long moment he sat there looking at Jessie with his eyes wider than I'd ever seen them. They were still wide when he said, "Well, maybe you should have thought about that before you turned me on, little woman," he said as quick as a jack rabbit.

Then Jessie roasted him, "Well, then you should get control of yourself, right?"

"Okay then. You win."

"Yeah, that's kind of how it always is and always will be."

That was when Dan yelled, "What, no!" and began to tickle Jessie, saying "No, no, that's not how it will be. I will win. I will always win." We all broke out laughing. Which I think reminded them that we were there. Because when we did, they both stopped what they were doing and looked at us stupidly embarrassed. Which was the main reason I was laughing because they're faces were so funny looking at us, like we scared the jeepers out of them both. But they started to smile again, softly, when they turned and looked back at each other.

"Well, I better get going now," Jessie said, looking so sweetly at Dan.

"All right, wanna meet tomorrow somewhere? Your pick."

Jessie looked up for a short moment before saying, "You can come to my place for breakfast at 6:35 a.m. if you want."

"Sounds good to me, my little woman," Dan said, giving Jessie a hug.

"Hahaha, not yet your little woman," Jessie said, before giving Dan a light kiss on the cheek. Dan smiled as Jessie jogged to her car.

"Bye, Jessie!"

"Bye, Danny!" Jessie shouted as she waved.

I noticed Mark waving at her, till John slapped his hand and said, "She's not waving at you, idiot. She's obviously waving at Dan." But Mark just stuck his tongue at him after he turned around.

"Well, big man, you finally have a girlfriend," Alex said.

Dan smirked and said, "I hope you know it's not cute when you say it," as he rubbed his hand on Alex's head.

"Yeah, finally not lonely in this whole wide world anymore. How does that feel?" Bradley yelled.

"I wasn't lonely, I was just…busy, that's all" Dan said, turning around, and opened his truck door.

"Whatever you say, Dan," Matt said, smirking at him.

"So what now?" I asked as Alex and I hopped in the bed of Dan's truck.

"I'm going home and finishing these papers for the motorcycle," Dan said, putting the papers in the air.

"What are those papers for, Dan?" Mark asked, getting more than a buzz from drinking. Dan didn't repeat himself but just looked up at him with his eyes then looked back at his papers.

"So then the cops know that they gave the motorcycle to me," Dan said, still looking closely at the papers.

"You're getting a motorcycle, Dan? How much was it?" George asked.

"Yes, the owner just gave it to me because he didn't have enough money for us to fix it. I told him I've never driven a motorcycle before. So he gave it to me anyways, and I don't even know what to do with it," Dan said, throwing the papers in the truck.

"If I were you, I would just sell it, so then you don't have to do the papers," Clark said.

"That's not a bad idea, Clark," Dan said, starting to smile.

Then Matt said, "Me, Bradley, and Mark are going to watch a movie at the movie house if you, Alex, and George want to come with us" as he walking on the other side of Dan where me, Alex, and George were. We looked at each other. Then I said, "Sure, we'll go with you guys," as we jumped off the side of Dan's truck. And said goodbye to Dan and the rest of the gang and started to walk to the movie.

When we got there it was packed, and I mean packed. It looked like there was more than two hundred people in cars and seats. "You guys go and find us some seats, while me, Bradley, and Mark go get something to eat and drink," Matt said, going into the movie concession stand.

"That's if we can," George said, already looking around for some in the back.

"I don't see any," Alex said, acting like he had binoculars.

"Me neither," I said, doing the same.

"I see some over there," George said, pointing at six seats on the left side of us. We tried to get there before anyone else did. But then five girls beat us. And George got mad and started to cuss them out. But then one of the girls said, "We've been waiting to see this movie all of last week."

"Oh…um…never mind, we'll just find another spot to sit," George said as he turned around, all bummed out.

"Oh, it's okay, George, we'll just sit in the bottom row," I said, trying to cheer him up.

"But that's why I started to cuss them out so we didn't have to sit at the bottom row so our neck doesn't hurt, but now I just feel like I'm the worst boy in the whole wide world for being so greedy about stupid seats," George said, folding his arms like he's getting yelled at or cold.

"You're not the worst boy in the world, George. The worst boy in the world is Black Fredrick," Alex said, patting George on the back.

"I guess you're right, but I still feel bad that I cussed those girls out," George said, looking back at them. "We know you are, but they probably don't care anymore, George. Now let's find some seats before Matt and them get back," I said, walking down the stairs.

We finally found seats before they got back with the popcorns and Pepsis. "Did you call Dad and tell him we're watching a movie?" I asked Matt as I passed the popcorn to Alex and George.

Matt looked at me as if confused. "Well, no," he said as he stuffed popcorn in his mouth like usual.

"What?" I yelled, and a whole bunch of people shushed me and told me to be more quiet. Even Alex and George.

"It will be fine, we'll be home before dinner is ready," Matt said, assuring me. I looked at Matt with a serious look on my face.

"Okay, I just don't want Dad to start yelling at us and tell us… well, me. You know how he is, Matt," I said.

"Yeah, I know how he is, but he's like that only with you because you're still young and can end up—"

Mark interrupted Matt and finished it for him. "Like me, Mike. A drinker, a smoker, and a cold-hearted young man." Then he paused to looked at me, making sure I was still listening, and then continued. "That's why your dad yells at you, because he doesn't want you to end up where I am or like Blake Frederick. Because he's protective over you, which means he loves you, and he wants the best for you."

Then he turned back around to watch the movie. "Oh yeah, he sure loves me more, now that Mom's gone," I said, being sarcastic. But no one laughed. "Oh wait, I meant he hates me now that Mom's gone."

"Michael, how could you say that when Dad told you this morning that he was proud of you for getting all As and Bs when you had a C-, D-, A, F, and a B- in the beginning of the year?" Matt yelled till a bunch of people shushed him. But he continued to make me feel ashamed of myself for a while. "I'm sorry, Mike, it's just I'm tired of you saying how much Dad hates you. When really, it's you who hates him. Which, you need to stop saying 'cause he's the only parent you have left and the only parent who's really proud of you," Matt said, making me feel even more ashamed of myself for thinking that my own dad just hates me after his wife died. But I should have known that he was just doing it to protect me from ending up as a drinker, a smoker, but I knew I was a cold-hearted young man for what I thought about my own dad and my only parent.

After the movie we all walked to mine and Matt's house to see what our dad was cooking tonight. "Man, that was sure one scary movie," George said with his hands in his pockets.

"Oh, was it, little brother?" Bradley said, jumping on George.

"Get off me, Bradley," George said as his legs started to get wobbly.

"Not until you give me a piggyback ride for two and a half blocks," Bradley said, pointing down the street.

"But you're too heavy for me to carry that far though," George said, trying to look at his brother, who was on his back.

"Fine, killjoy," Bradley said, hopping off George's back.

"Hey, you okay, little man?" Matt said, running over to me. "I'm sorry that I got mad at you in front of your friends," he said, putting one arm around me.

"It's not that. You just made me realize how mean I was to Dad, and I was mean, you know," I said.

"Yeah, I know you were."

When we stepped into the house, Dad and Dan were the only ones in the house, eating dinner. Which is odd. Because usually the whole gang is eating in our living room, watching television. "Where is everybody?" Bradley asked, looking around.

"Well, John went to his mother's house because she wasn't feeling too good. David wasn't feeling like coming over. Mark and Clark's mom and dad had dinner ready for Clark," Dad said, grabbing his food, which was spaghetti.

"What were they having?" Mark asked with curiosity.

"All they said on the telephone was that it was your favorite," Dad said as he ate some of his spaghetti.

"Holy moly, I got to go," Mark said, running out the door.

"Well, I better get home to my folks, Mr. D," Alex said, opening the door back up.

"Okay, see ya, Alex," Dad said, waving at him.

"George and I will stay here and help eat your spaghetti, Mr. D," Bradley said, walking into the kitchen with George following him.

"Okay," Dad said chuckling. And Matt and I got in line for Dad's spaghetti. After dinner, I just threw some pajama pants on and went to bed.

CHAPTER 5

When I woke up, it was 6:30 a.m. So I decided to take a long, hot shower. I grabbed a pair of my pants and socks with a plain white T-shirt then hopped in the shower. This was the first time I woke up before everyone else. Usually Dad's the first one up and makes breakfast.

When I got out, I threw my clothes on and brushed my teeth and combed my hair. When I got out of the bathroom, I grabbed my sneakers, slipped them on by the couch, and started to make breakfast for Matt and Dad. I decided to make pancakes and eggs. Our rule in the house for the first person that woke up is that you make breakfast. But you at least get to choose what everyone eats. Once I got the eggs done and started to make the pancakes, I heard the door creak open and shut. Then Dan walked into the kitchen.

"Hey, little brother, what are you making?" he asked, grabbing a cup and look in the fridge.

"Pancakes and eggs. Do you want some?" I asked and turned around, watching him pour milk into his cup.

"Oh no, I'm fine, Mike. I had breakfast at Jessie's house, but thanks," he said before he chugged the milk down.

"You ate at her house?" I said, turning around to look at him chiefly.

"Yep, and it was a nice house too," he said, putting the cup in the sink.

"Can we go over there?" I asked duly.

"The whole gang?" Dan asked with a concerned look on his face.

"No, just me, you, and Matt," I said, turning back to the pancake I was cooking.

"She probably wouldn't mind."

"We'll go there once Dad wakes up." Right when I said that, Dad walked into the living room.

"Why are you up so early, little man?" Dad said, putting on his jacket.

"I just woke up early and started to make pancakes," I said, putting the pancake that I was cooking on a plate.

"Okay, well, I got to go to work in ten minutes. So I'll eat some of your pancakes and eggs that you made and get out of here," Dad said, grabbing a plate from the cupboards.

"All right, sounds good," I said, putting some pancake mix on the pan.

"Hey, what's cooking and who's cooking it?" Matt said, peeking around the corner.

"Pancakes and eggs," I said, flipping the pancake that was in the pan.

"Ooh, yummy," Matt said, getting a plate.

"Oh, Matt. do you want to go to Jessie's house with me and Dan?" I said, turning to look at him.

"Heck yeah!" Matt said, stuffing pancakes and eggs in his mouth.

Then the door creaked again, and I heard a whole bunch of footsteps coming in all at once. And that was when I knew that it was the gang walking into our house. "Hey, I didn't know you could cook, Mike" Mark said, walking into the kitchen.

"It's pancakes. Pancakes are easy to make, anyone can make pancakes, you dummy," John said, glaring at him.

"Why don't you laugh. It's good to laugh once in a while, it's even healthy for you, did you know that?" Mark said, trying to make him crack a smile. John hardly smiles since his girlfriend, Marcy, died in a car crash. I think because he was thinking about marrying her. But then the worst happened, and someone was speeding and ran into her and flipped her car. After that, no one could make him laugh at all. His laughter and joy left his heart. But his pride didn't, and now his heart is filled with pain and anger.

"Hey, do you guys want to go to Jessie's house with us after we're done eating?" Matt asked them as he sat at the table.

"Sure, if Dan doesn't mind," David said, getting his food.

"I don't care, it's Jess who might care," Dan said, sounding irritated.

"I think she wouldn't mind, and if she does, we'll just say we begged you," Bradley said, getting his food.

"All right then, hurry up and eat and then we'll go," Dan said, walking into the living room.

"All right, big man," Mark said, going to sit next to Matt.

"You guys are just going to keep teasing me about that the rest of our lives, aren't you?"

"Well, you don't seem to mind, do ya?"

We all started to walk out of the house when Dad did. "See you guys at 4:30 p.m.," Dad said, throwing his work bag in his little red truck.

"See you, Mr. D," George said, waving at him.

"So what was she making when you came to her house?" I asked as we stared to walk there.

"Oh, she had doughnuts at her house, and they were good too," Dan said with a curious look on his face.

"She has doughnuts at her house," Mark said, trying to light a cigarette.

"Yep, she has chocolate, sprinkled, filling ones, and all kinds of doughnuts. And the best part is that they're all homemade," Dan said.

"Please stop, you're making my stomach growl, Dan," Bradley said, rubbing his stomach.

"Okay," Dan said, chuckling.

When we got there, you could hear her listen to the song "Such a Night" by Elvis Presley. "Man, she must love Elvis's music," Alex said as we walked up her steps. Dan knocked on the door, and the music went down. We could still hear it though. You could also hear every step she took until she got to the door and opened it. She was wearing a worn-out jean jacket that was almost buttoned all the way but was tied in a knot at the bottom. She was also wearing old shorts. She wore her hair up in a messy bun with two curls on each side of her face with white and blue paint spattered from her head to toe. My guess was that she was painting.

"Hey, you guys. What are you doing here?" she said, opening the door wider.

"We just wanted to come and say hi," Dan said.

"Oh okay, come on in," she said, moving out of the doorway.

"So where's the doughnuts?" Mark said, rubbing his hands together.

"Is that what you came here for, Mark?" Jessie said.

"What, no, silly," Mark said, making a weird face.

Then she gave him a mom look.

"Okay, maybe I came here for just the doughnuts," he said, shrugging.

"They're in the cupboard," she said, pointing at the cupboard.

"Okay, thanks, Jessie," Mark said, walking into her kitchen.

"So what are you two going to do today?" David asked, walking into the kitchen with Mark.

"Well, I don't work today. So I guess I'll go to the park with Romeo, if I can find him," she said, looking around.

"Who's Romeo again?" Bradley asked. That was when Romeo came trampling into the living room and tackled Bradley.

"Oh my goodness," Jessie said, putting a hand to her mouth. "I'm so sorry, Bradley, he gets overly excited when meeting new people," Jessie said, taking Romeo off Bradley.

For a moment, Bradley sat on the ground, laughing like a cow before he said, "It's okay, Jessie, I'm fine," as he cracked up. Jessie gave him an odd look.

"Are you sure?" she asked.

"Yeah, you kinda look like you're possessed," Dan said. Then Bradley passed out. "Hey, hey, buddy, you okay?" Dan said, shaking him. John bent down next to Dan. They both got closer to Bradley until he yelled, "Ahh!" Dan and John both jumped back. Dan began to laugh, while John got up and said, "Gosh damn, you scared the living shit out of me!" Dan got up, and Bradley sat on the floor, laughing.

"Can someone help me up?"

John looked down at him and yelled, "*No!* Help yourself."

As John and Bradley bickered, Dan asked, "So where do you want to walk him?"

Jessie drew her eyes to the ceiling to think. "How about we go to the park and see what we want to do from there," Jessie said as she turned her gaze on Dan.

"Sounds good to me," Dan said as he walked over to her.

"What else sounds good to you?" she said, turning toward him.

"Doughnuts," he said, smiling. But she just giggled and walked into the kitchen. "Hey, where are you going? I'm not done talking to you, little miss," Dan said, following her.

"Going to get a drink, why?" she said, standing in the entrance of the kitchen.

"I just don't like it," Dan said.

Then I noticed that they were flirting with each other. And I guess the gang knew that too. "Ohh, look at you two, all in your own little world when you look in each other's eyes," Matt said, sounding girly as he fluttered his eye lids. But they just looked at him weirdly with a smile.

"I'll take a shower, get dressed, and then we can leave," Jessie said, getting a glass of water. After Jessie took a shower, got dressed and put a leash on Romeo, we all stepped out of the house and started to walk to the park.

"So tell me a little more about yourself," Dan said as he and Jessie swung their hands.

"I already told you all about me, Dan," Jessie said.

"You haven't told me what type of food is your favorite or what kind of music you like yet," Dan said.

"Well, I don't have a favorite food, but I like Paul McCartney, Freddie Mercury, Elvis Presley, Sam Cooke, Looking Glass, and a whole bunch of singers. But those are my favorite," she said.

"Really," Dan said with a smile.

"Yeah, why, are some of those your favorite too?" she said, smiling back.

"Yeah, actually," Dan said, smiling even more.

"We have a lot in common," she said.

"Like what?" George asked.

"Well, we like the same singers, we both like black coffee, we have brothers, we both hate cats and strawberries, we both work at a car and motorcycle shop…she continued. That's at least some of the things we have in common," she said, counting all the things they hate and like with her fingers.

"Wow, you do have a lot in common so far," Alex said.

We could tell they were in love just by looking at them. Even if they had only known each other for a day or two. But that didn't matter to them obviously. They were in love, and no one could break them apart. Kinda like Mom and Dad. They were so in love that it didn't matter what hit them. They would get through it together.

I remember Mom telling us how much her dad hated our dad and how he didn't care if he loved our mom. He loved her whether her dad liked it or not. But in the end, her dad accepted him, and they got married and had Dan, then Matt, and then me, Mike. Man, I miss our mom so much. I wish she got to live longer so she could see Dan find love and see Matt grow up to be a fine young man and see me in eleventh grade level after taking that long, boring test. But that's just how some things are. Hard, painful, and sad. Which can sometimes make you weaker or stronger and make you what you'll be in the future and what your life will be without them. Rich or poor, easy or hard, happy or sad, help you or haunt you, and get better or more terrible at some things. So pretty much life is just a test or maze or obstacle course or anything like that. You'll never know when something bad or good is going to happen till it happens, and you'll never know what's right or wrong until the end of it.

When we got to the park, there were a whole bunch of people. Even Chris and his friends were hanging out there. But when they saw us, they walked over to us, and Chris asked, "Why are you hanging out with these losers, pretty face?"

Then Jessie said, "Because they don't treat me like trash like you guys do, and he's my boyfriend too." She pointed at Dan.

And Ethan said, "Your boyfriend is a bum, sweet—"

Before he could finish, Jessie exploded and said, "He's not a bum, and neither are his brothers and friends, and if anyone's a loser, it's you guys. Little pucks that drive around beating up poor kids who have enough trouble going on in their lives. I feel truly sorry for your parents who raised you."

Bradley, Matt, and Mark burst out laughing as Mark said, "You just got told by a girl. No offense, Jess."

"Stop laughing, you—"

Then Jessie interrupted them again and said, "Don't call them whatever you were going to call them, and they can laugh at you all they want for what you do to them." She folded her arms.

Then they started to walk up to her, and we started walk up to them. "Don't you even dare," Dan said, glaring at them. They knew they couldn't take on all ten of us because they had half as many guys as we did.

So Chris said "This isn't over" as he turned around and walked off with his friends.

"You need to be a little more careful from now on," Dan said, turning toward Jessie.

"Why?" she said with a puzzled look.

"Because they'll jump you when you're alone," John said.

"Exactly, and they don't care who you are or what you are. They'll still jump you. So be careful when you go on a walk alone," Dan said, putting his hands on her shoulders.

"I will, don't worry, okay," she said as she hugged him.

"Okay," he said as he hugged her back. Then Dan noticed that we were looking at them and said, "What are you knuckleheads looking at?"

Bradley started to smirk. "Nothing, just you two lovebirds."

"We should go," Jessie said, letting go of Dan.

"Yeah, we should," Matt said.

We started to walk when Dan said, "I never thought you would ever say that to them." He wrapped his arm around Jessie.

"Well, why wouldn't I?" she asked.

"Because you were too sweet, at least that's what I thought," Dan said.

She cocked an eyebrow and said, "Well, you don't know me that well, Danny, remember?" She gave him a little smirk.

When we got to Jessie's house, you could tell that Dan didn't want to leave her there all alone, when you looked in his eyes. "Bye, boys," Jessie said as she got to the door.

"Bye, Jessie," Alex said, waving. Then we started to walk back to the house.

"Man, I hate leaving her there all alone," Dan said, looking tense.

"I think she'll be fine, Daniel," John said, patting him on the back.

"Yeah, don't worry, Chris and his friends aren't going to hurt her as long as that German shepherd's around," Mark said.

"I guess so," Dan said, still looking worried.

When we got to the house, we ate tuna fish sandwiches with chips as we watched television. "You really like her, huh, Dan," Matt said, looking at Dan with a smile.

"Like her? I love her," Dan said, smiling back at him.

"I would too if I were you. She's sweet, beautiful, and sticks up for what's right too. You're a lucky man, Dan," John said.

"Yeah, I guess I am," Dan said.

After Alex, George, and I got done eating, we decided to walk to town and back so we could kill time. "I never thought they would fall in love that quickly," Alex said.

"Me neither," George said, shaking his head.

"I'm glad they love each other, because Dan isn't lonely anymore," I said.

"You know what it means if they decide to be with each other, right," George said.

"Yeah, I know. But at least he's not lonely and is happy now," I said, smiling.

"Yeah, I guess you're right, Mike," Alex said.

"Yeah, you're a good little brother, Mike," George said, patting me on the back.

"Thanks, guys," I said.

Then someone honked their horn at us, and we turned around to see who it was. It was Chris and his friends again. You could tell they were looking for us by how fast they were going. They got closer and closer by every wild spin, and once they got close to us, they turned in front of us and got out.

"Well, well, well, look what the cat dragged in," Chris said, walking toward us.

"A bunch of little punks, Chris," Steven said, another friend of Chris.

"Again, we must get rid of them before the population grows," Chris said as they started to surround us.

Then a stern voice said, "Leave them alone." And they all turned around. It was my dad who said that. He looked all high and mighty with his chest all puffed up, and they all backed out of his way so he could grab us. When he did, Chris said, "You should be glad that your daddy came here in time."

And my dad said, "And you should be glad I didn't beat the tar out of you kid." We got in his truck and drove off. "Are you guys okay?" he asked.

"Yeah, we're fine, Mr. D," George said contentedly.

"They're really scared of you, Mr. D," Alex said with a grin.

"Probably because I'm old and mean," Dad said.

"Yeah, you're right, you are old and mean," George said, being sarcastic.

When we got home, I was about to get out of the car when Dad said, "Stay here, I want to talk to you, Mike."

When he said that, I thought I was in trouble for something but couldn't think of anything I did. When Alex and George ran in the house, Dad asked, "So what's going on with you?"

"What do you mean?" I asked, almost terrified.

"I mean, why are you so sad all of a sudden when you see me?" he said, looking at me all worriedly.

"It's just that I'm feeling ashamed of myself."

"Why would you feel ashamed of yourself?" Dad said, looking all confused.

"Well, because...I thought you hated me and loved Dan and Matt more than me. But then Matt told me the only reason why you yell at me is because you're protective over me and love me and how proud you are of me and don't want to lose me. And here I've been thinking my own dad hates me when he actually just loves me more than anything and anyone," I said, feeling like I was going to start crying.

"Oh, little Mike, it's okay. I can see why you would think that," he said. That was the first time in forever since he called me little Mike. "I guess I was too hard on you after your mom died and wasn't thinking of what it did to you. I'm sorry," Dad said.

Then I said, "No, I'm sorry for everything I thought about you, Dad."

Then dad just smiled and said, "It's okay, little man." He rubbed my head.

After that, we went inside. Dad started to cook dinner, and I started getting ready to take a shower. "So what did you and your dad talk about?" George asked as he and Alex walked into my bedroom.

"Dad and son problems that are now fixed," I said, grabbing pajamas.

"Oh, that's good," Alex said, smiling.

"Yeah, I'm glad we talked. I couldn't stand feeling ashamed of myself," I said, walking into the bathroom.

"Hey, Mike!" Dad yelled from the kitchen.

"Yeah?" I yelled back.

"Don't take a shower yet. Dinner's almost done, okay."

"Okay," I said, walking out of the bathroom.

"So what are we having for dinner today, Mr. D?" George asked as he walked into the kitchen.

"Well, George, we're having pulled pork sandwiches," Dad said.

"Sounds good, Mr. D," David said, walking into the kitchen.

After we all ate, I took a hot shower and got dressed. When I got out of the bathroom, the gang had left, and Matt was cleaning the dishes. "So how's Jessie doing, Dan?" Dad asked as he went to sit on the couch.

"Good, I might go over to see her after I leave," Dan said, smiling.

"Oh, that's good, Dan, I'm happy for you. You finally found a good girl," Dad said, smiling back.

CHAPTER 6

The next morning, Dad had gone to work, and the gang was at the house eating breakfast already. I guess I woke up a little late this time. But for some reason, Dan wasn't there. Usually he's at the house, waiting for us to get done eating our breakfast so we could play football at the park. "Where's Dan?" I asked, rubbing my face.

"He stayed at Jessie's house," John said, getting up off the couch.

"Really?" I said, getting a glass of milk.

"Yeah, but he didn't sleep in the same bed with her," David said, walking out of the hall.

"Is he coming over here?" I asked before I took a drink of the glass of milk.

"I don't know," John said, leaning against the counter.

"Oh well, we can play football without him," Mark said, taking a drink of his beer.

"But we never play football without him, and it will be uneven too," Alex said, complaining.

"He won't care, and we can just have one person out till one of the teams get a touchdown and switch," Clark said.

"Fine," Alex said.

When we got to the park, Dan and Jessie were there. Like they knew we were coming.

"Hey, you guys," Jessie said once she saw us.

"Hey, how did you know we were coming here?" Bradley said.

"Oh, we didn't. We just came here to walk Romeo," she said, smiling at us.

"Oh yeah, I knew that," Bradley said, making her smile even more.

"No, you didn't," Dan said, making a weird face.

"Maybe, maybe not," Bradley said, shrugging.

"Do you want to play football with us, Daniel?" John asked, throwing the football in the air.

"Um..." Dan said, looking at Jessie.

"Oh, come on, go play football with the gang, Dan. I need to go anyways," she said, pushing him toward us.

"Okay, okay, come on, let's go play some football, you guys," Dan said, smiling like never before.

"Bye, Dan, have fun," she said, waving.

"I will, bye, love you," Dan said, waving back.

"Uh, Dan, you love her," Matt said, hugging him.

"Of course I love her. Now get off of me, Matt," Dan said.

"Okay, Danny poo," Matt said, letting go of him.

"Thank you, now let's go play some football," Dan said, taking the ball out of John's hands and running to where we play football.

"Ready, set, hike!" Dan yelled. All of us started to scatter everywhere on the field and running into each other. No one could get a touchdown though. No matter what they did. So we just gave up and called it a day. We were all breathing really hard. But at least it was raining, so we weren't breathing too hard.

"Man, what a game," George said, trying to catch his breath.

"Yeah, no one could get a touchdown," Alex said, putting his jacket on.

"It was fun though," I said, slouching.

"Yeah, it was," Bradley said, interrupting our talk.

"Come on, let's get out of the rain," Dan said, and we all followed him.

"So where are we going to go, Dan?" David asked.

"Well, I'm probably going to go to my house. If you guys want to come with, you can," Dan said.

"Got no problem with that. I'm bored sitting here," David said. We all walked to Dan's house.

His house wasn't as big as Dad's house or as small as old people's houses are. It was a medium-size house with one bedroom, one bathroom, and a living room that can fit eight people in it. Dan's house wasn't that good-looking either. But it was home to him. Dan once told me that it didn't matter what your house looked like in the outside. The only thing that matters is that you have a roof over your head, a warm place to stay, and it's dry inside. So now I know what kind of house to look for when I get older.

Once we got to Dan's house, we immediately started to look for food. But there was nothing in his house, so we went next door and took some of Dad's food and went back to Dan's house. "Did you just go next door and steal some food?" Dan said, glaring at us.

"Well yeah," Bradley said.

"Why?" Dan asked.

"What do you mean 'why'?" Bradley said.

"He means, why did you steal some food from next door," John said.

"Because he barely has food in his house!" Mark shouted, sounding skeptical.

"Calm down, you guys, geez," Dan said dramatically.

"Okay," John, Bradley, and Mark said at the same time.

"Thank you," Dan said. After we were done eating, we took the rest of the food back, and we all stayed at Dad's house and watched some television. The kind of shows and sitcoms we liked to watch are *Cheers*, *Night Court*, *The Cosby Show*, *M*A*S*H**, and *Who's the Boss*. And the kind that are funny or have to do with the army.

When Dad got home, he was carrying bags of food in his hands. "Can you boys get the rest of the food, please," Dad said, and we started to walk out the door.

"What did you get, Mr. D?" Alex asked, looking in one of the bags.

"Food, of course," Mark said, grinning.

"I knew that, Mark," Alex said, grabbing more bags.

"Oh, you did? I thought you didn't know when you asked 'What did you get?'" Mark said, walking into the house with Alex.

"What did you get, Dad?" I asked as he walked over to get more bags of food.

"Like Mark said, food," he said, smiling at me, and I smiled back at him as I grabbed some bags of food.

"What kind though?" Matt said, looking in some of the bags with curiosity.

"You'll see when we get all the bags in the house. Unless you'd rather peek in every bag, Matt," Dad said as he stopped on the porch.

"What?" Matt asked, turning around to look at Dad.

"Just grab as many bags as you can, Matt." Dad sighed as he started to walk in the house.

"Okay, Dad," Matt said as he grabbed a whole bunch of bags. Once we got all the bags in the house, we started to put everything where they belonged. "You got cake mix, for what, Dad?" Matt asked as he looked at the cake mix.

"Probably because it's almost our little brother's birthday next Friday, knucklehead," Dan said, giving me one of his bear hugs.

"Oh, that's right, I totally forgot. I'm sorry, little brother," Matt said, wrapping his arm around me and Dan.

"It's fine, we still have ten days till my birthday," I said, putting my hands in my pockets.

"I know, but I should know my own little brother's birthday, now should I," he said, taking his arm off me.

"I guess so," I said.

"Mike, hurry up and get out of the shower before your dinner gets cold," Dad said, standing on the other side of the door.

"I'm getting out right now," I said, turning off the shower.

"All right, I'll leave a plate out for you," Dad said.

"Okay, thanks," I said, stepping out of the shower.

"You're welcome," Dad said as he walked away from the door. I hurried up and slipped on my pajamas, combed my hair, then walked out of the bathroom. My food was sitting on the table. It was a hot-dog with potato salad. I grabbed it and sat on the couch, watching *The Cosby Show* with the gang.

"I need to go to my mom's house and stay with her tonight," John said, getting up off the couch.

"Is she getting better?" David asked.

"Not really," John said.

"I'm sorry, John," Alex said.

"It's okay, it's not like I never lost someone before, you know," John said, putting on his shoes.

"Bye, John, tell your mom we said hi," Dad said, putting the leftovers in the icebox.

"I will," John said, opening the door.

"Bye, John," Dan said.

"Bye, Dan," John said, walking out the door.

Once he shut it, George said, "I feel bad for him. He lost his girlfriend and now he might lose his mom too."

"I know, let's just not talk about it, okay," Dan said, getting off the couch.

"Okay," Alex said.

"Well, I need to go too," Mark said, getting up off the floor. When he left, everyone left the house. Dan went to his house, Mark and Clark went back home, Bradley and George went back home too, and so did Alex. And the house got quiet, and we all decided to go to bed at 9:30 p.m.

CHAPTER 7

"Hey, wake up, we have school today, Mike," Matt said, shaking me awake.

"Okay, okay, I'll get up, just..." I started to stretch. "Just give me five more minutes," I said, trying to go back to sleep.

"No, get up now, little man, it's six o'clock already. You gotta be at school in twenty minutes. So get up," Dad said, coming in my bedroom.

"Okay, I'm getting up. Now leave me alone," I said, throwing the blankets off me.

"All right, get dressed while I make breakfast for you and Matt," Dad said as he and Matt walked out and shut the door. I wanted to lay down and go back to sleep.

But I knew I would make myself and Matt late for school and Dad late for work. So I'd rather get up than have them get mad at me for making them late for school and work. I put on a pair of jeans and socks, a T-shirt, and a plaid flannel. Then made my bed and walked out of my bedroom. Once I did, there was this great smell of ham and eggs in the air. When I walked into the kitchen, yhere were two plates of ham and eggs sitting on the counter for me and Matt. "Thanks, Dad," I said, grabbing my plate.

"Yeah, thanks," Matt said, grabbing his plate.

"You're welcome, boys," Dad said, walking out of the kitchen with us. Then Alex walked into the house.

"Hey, Alex, why are you here?" Matt asked as he sat down at the table.

"My dad's car broke down," he said, panting.

"Did you run here?" I asked.

"Yes, I did. Do you think you can give me a ride to school, Mr. D?" he asked, still panting.

"Yeah, I will, don't worry, and take in deep breaths, okay, son," Dad said, patting him on the back so hard that it seemed to knock the wind out of him.

"Thanks, Mr. D," Alex said.

"No problem," Dad said.

We hopped in Dad's little red truck and drove off. "I'll drop you boys off then drive to work," Dad said.

"Sounds good, Dad," Matt said, putting on his seatbelt. Matt, Alex, and I are usually the first ones at school. It's probably because we're closer to the school. My dad's house is about six or seven blocks away from the school. Alex's parents' house is about ten or eleven. Mark and Clark's mom and stepdad's house is about fourteen or fifteen. George and Bradley's mom's house is about eighteen or nineteen. And David's dad's house is about twenty-two or twenty-three. When we got to school, we said goodbye to my dad before he speeded to work. One time he was really late to work and was speeding and a cop pulled him over. So he was even more late for work. He hasn't got pulled over since. Probably because he's getting old and old people don't drive so fast when they hit their forties. Matt said because they're getting more old and wise at the age of forty. Dad is already forty-one years old but is grumpy and is kind of wise, I guess.

Matt, Alex, and I waited for the rest of the gang to get there, at the entrance of the school, for about ten minutes until they came racing to school.

"Hey, you guys, excited for school today?" Bradley said as he ran up the steps to us.

"Oh yeah, and I'm so happy to go to school today," I said sarcastically.

"Ohh, really, you don't sound like it." He chuckled.

"Probably because I was being sarcastic."

"I think none of us are excited or happy to go to school today. It's Tuesday," Alex said.

"That's right, I forgot it was Memorial Day on Monday," David said as we started to walk in the school. David is a year behind in school. Only because he didn't want to go to school; he'd rather drink. But hey, that's all in his past now, and no one dares talk about it. I mean *no one*!

When we walked up to the school doors, we saw Chris and his friends bullying the new kid that came to school about a month ago. I felt bad for him. I wanted to help him, but I knew we would start a fistfight, and we would all have a detention or get suspended, and our parents will probably get mad at us and will not let us hang out with each other anymore.

So I ignored them. "I can't wait for school to get out," George said when we got to our lockers.

"Me too, I'm getting tired of all this homework and stuff," I said.

"Me three, because…well, I don't know why, but I'm sure excited for it to get out," Alex said as we started to walk to our first class. Alex, George, and I all have the same classes besides our elective class. I have writing class, Alex has wood shop, and George has auto mechanics. But we all had gym one semester.

My classes went, ELA, math, writing class, history, then science. My favorite class is ELA. Not just because Alex George, and I sit next to each other, but because our teacher, Mrs. Wells, is the nicest teacher out of all my classes. She lets us talk five minutes before we get out and lets us use a book for a test. She first lets us take notes out of the book. Then when we take the test, she lets us use the book if we want to. But of course, we all use the book, and after we're done with the test, she lets us do whatever we want as long as we are quiet.

"Hello, my favorite class, today we're not going to do much. First we are going to read for twenty minutes, then you can do whatever you want, like finish homework in other classes, talk to friends, or you can keep on reading if you want," she said, and we all got to reading. I was reading *The Outsiders*, Alex was reading *The Unbearable Lightness of Being*, and George was reading Stephen King's *The Eye of the Dragon*. For some reason, George likes scary books. He already read all the Stephen King series. One time I read one of the books, and it made me almost jump out of my chair. Alex likes adventure books. I like any kind of book as long as it isn't scary, like George's kind of books.

"Okay, class, time is up. Go ahead and do whatever you want as long as you are quiet," she said, and we all immediately started to talk as quiet as possible. But our class was big, so it was kind of hard to keep things down. She knew that, so she shut the door to her classroom.

"So what should we talk about, you guys?" George asked, trying to take his eyes off his book.

"I'm on chapter nine," I said, trying to start a conversation.

"I forgot what chapter I'm on," Alex said, looking through his book.

George flashed a smile as he shook his head at Alex. "Oh, Alex, Alex, Alex."

Alex looked at him. "What?"

"You're just so complicated, that's all."

"Yeah, I know I'm complicated," Alex said.

"I think we all know that, Alex," I said.

"Yeah, probably," he said.

Then we got back to reading because we didn't have anything to talk about. After Mrs. Well's, we go to Mr. Clan's classroom, who's the meanest teacher of all time. Like if he calls on you and you get it wrong, he'll keep calling on you until you get an answer right. Also, he will wear black if we are going to take a test, which is kind of nice of him to do because that's when you know that today is a test day. But he doesn't tell you that it is a test day, not even when he hands it out to you. You just got to remember that if he wears black, like he's going to a funeral, that today is a test day. After his class, I go to Ms. Jean's class, which is my second favorite class. She doesn't yell at us as much as Mr. Clean. But she still yells at us. Especially when we get too loud or when we aren't listening to her instructions. After her class, I go to Ms. Dalton and Ms. McClam, which are my second and third least favorite classes.

After school, we missed the bus because we decided to call Jessie to ask if she could come and pick us up. "Yeah, I can, I'll be there in ten minutes," she said.

"Okay, thanks, Jessie," I said.

"No problem, Mike."

So we sat there, waiting for her at the curb to pick us up. Then Chris and his friends walked up to us. George glared at them. "What do you want, rich kids?" he said angrily. George gets this way when he's scared or is trying to be tough.

"We want to know why you bums are still here at this trashy school," Dusty said.

"Don't you go to this school too?" Alex asked.

"Listen here, little punks, tell your big punk brother that his girlfriend is going to get it for—"

"For what, telling you off?" George teased. That's when Jessie pulled up in her little red Chevy Impala and yelled, "Are you bugging them?"

"Why do you care?" Ethan asked.

"Because they're my boyfriend's little brothers and his friends, that's why. So you better leave them alone."

They all turned to her. "Or what, he'll try to beat us up?" Chris asked.

"No, I will. So let them and me be so we can leave, okay," she said, giving them sauce. "Now come on in my car and let's get out of here."

We jumped in the car and drove off, leaving them in the dust.

"Can we go to your house?" George asked.

"Sure, I don't care. But why are they like that?" she asked very angrily.

"What do you mean?" I asked.

"Why are they always trying to pick up a fight with you guys?"

"Well, they're the rich kids, and we are the not-so-rich kids," Alex said.

"And that gives them the right to be bullies?" she asked, getting angrier.

"Well, yeah, I guess."

"So you're telling me that the only reason why they pick up fights with you is because they're rich and you're the not-so-rich?"

"Yep," I said, nodding my head up and down.

"That's the most stupid thing I ever heard in my entire life."

"Yeah, I know," I said.

"I wish I could do something, but you know, I'm a girl, and what's a girl going to do to a bunch of teenage boys, I mean, I'm not that strong," she said, starting to calm down.

"That's not true, Jessie," George blurted. "You're stronger than you think. Just in a different way. Your greatest strength is kindness, and kindness is the strongest thing in the world. Because if someone shows people enough kindness, those people will stand by your side when you're in need." We looked at him with shock in our eyes.

"Wow," Jessie said with an amazed expression. "I mean, thank you."

When we got to her house, we ate some doughnuts with chocolate milk. And those doughnuts were delicious. Some were chocolate, maple with sprinkles on it. Some were filled with chocolate, vanilla, and raspberry. After eating five or six doughnuts, I finally asked, "How did you make these doughnuts so good?"

"Well, it took me a while to make them this good, but once you learn how to make them, you know exactly what makes them taste good."

"Really, do you think you could teach us how to make them?" George asked, licking the frosting off his fingers.

"Sure, but not today. I used all the stuff to make them."

"Okay," I said, turning on the television. Her television was pretty big. It was like Dad's but just bigger and fancier. Then Matt, David, Bradley, Mark, and Clark came in.

"Why are you little boys here?" Bradley asked.

"We asked if we could go to her house when she picked us up from school. Now why are you here?" George said, giving Bradley a sassy look.

"Well, we thought we would come over here and say hi. Do you have a problem with that, little brother?"

"I was wondering the same thing, big brother." George started to smirk at his big brother. Bradley just smiled back and walked up to Jessie. "Hey, what are you going to make for dinner, Jess?"

"Oh, I don't know. But I got to think of something because my brothers are coming over. That means you can't stay here long because they'll ask me a bunch of questions about you."

"Oh man," Bradley said, snapping his fingers.

"I'm sorry."

"It's fine, I can just eat at Mr. D's house."

She gave him an odd glare then asked, "Whose Mr. D?"

"He's your boyfriend's dad. We call him that because he has the same name as Dan," Mark said, holding a beer in his hands.

"When will you ever stop drinking, Mark?" I asked.

"Maybe when I get married or when I have kids. But until then, I'm going to keep drinking even if it kills me." He held up his beer then took a drink of it. We all just laughed. Jessie just shook her head at him and smiled.

Then Dan walked in. "What are you knuckleheads doing here?" he asked as he shut the door.

"'Cause they can be here, not just you, Danny," Jessie said meaningfully to him.

"Oh, sorry, I didn't know, my lady," he said, starting to bow to her.

Jessie hoisted an eyebrow and gathered her arms to her chest to say, "Daniel."

Dan immediately stood straight to say, as if baffled, "What? Something wrong, my lady?"

"Yeah, your dirty shoes."

Then he looked down and said, "They're not that dirty." Jess presented him a very overwhelming look that even made me feel like I was in trouble for some reason. "Okay, I'll take them off," he said, groaning.

"You need to start remembering or I'll just put a sign on the door that says, 'Take off your shoes, Daniel Herman,'" she said and pointed to the door.

"I'm sorry, I'm getting Alzheimer's, you know." He took off his shoes.

"You are not getting Alzheimer's, Dan, you are only twenty-one years old."

"Yes, I am."

"No, you're not."

"Yes, I am, Jess, I swear to you that I am."

"No, you're not, you're too young to have Alzheimer's," she said, laughing.

"Fine, I don't, but I forget a lot though."

"I know you forget a lot, but I still love you," she said, putting her arms around his rib cage.

"Aww, you love me?" He was sticking his lip out at her.

"Yeah, I love you. Now do you love me, or did you forget whether you love me or not too?" she said as they pulled each other closer with every baby step.

"Oh come on, you know I love you," Dan said, looking like he was about to kiss her. But to be honest, you can't blame him. Jessie's lips had a kissable look to them and had a natural puffy look too. It was not only her lips that might make him wanna smooch her, but her big round-shaped eyes. Big round eyes seem to have a more sweet, lovable, gentle look to them. As if they were a cuddly puppy or a happy chubby baby. Now tell me who wouldn't want to kiss a chubby baby or at least hold it tight in your arms.

After a moment passed of Dan and Jess whispering to each other, while the boys and I went on to the comfort of the couch, Bradley yelled, "Get a room, there's children around here!" He was pointing at Alex, George, and me. They both looked at him with a smile.

"Sorry, he forgot you guys were there," Jessie said, letting go of him.

"What do you mean 'him'?" Dan chuckled.

"Well, didn't you just say you forget a lot?" she said as she squinted at him.

"I did say that, didn't I?"

"Yep."

"Damn it," Dan whispered.

"Excuse you, Daniel. There's kids around here, or did you forget about them again."

"Sorry, my lady." Dan hee-hawed.

"You better be."

When Jessie got done cooking dinner for her brothers, we started to get ready to leave. "I'm so sorry you can't stay."

Then Dan said as he walked up to her, "Oh, don't worry, Jess, it's fine, I'll just come back tomorrow."

"They're staying here," she said.

"Then we'll meet at the park tomorrow, okay," he said as he kissed her forehead.

Mark yelled, "Hey, no kiss when there's children around!" He pointed at them.

"It was her forehead, and they're not children, Mark, they're teenagers," Dan said, giving him a nasty look.

"You still kissed her, and they're still children," Mark said, trying to be funny.

When Dan went to open the door, it flew open to reveal five guys standing on the steps with their wives and kids. Once the person that threw the door open saw us, he glared real hard at us. "Who are you guys!" he said in a very angry voice. We stood there by the door, looking at each other like a bunch of dummies.

"Answer me!" he yelled.

"Well, this is my…um…boyfriend," Jessie said, popping out from behind us.

"Boyfriend!" they all yelled.

"Yep, and his name is Daniel, but you can call him Dan," Jessie said.

"What's his last name?" one of them asked.

"Herman," she said.

"Do you love her?" he said as he started to walk up the stairs to Dan.

"Well, of course I love her, but not just her looks but her personality, and she brings the kid back in me," Dan said, smiling at Jessie.

"Okay, that's all I need to know," he said, stepping into the house. "Oh, I almost forgot, I'm Jason by the way," he said, shaking Dan's hand. "The nice one." He smirked at Dan. They all started to walk in, one by one, glaring at Dan.

Once they walked in and saw us, one of them asked, "If he's your boyfriend, then who are they?"

"Oh, these are Dan's brothers, Matt and Mike." She pointed at Matt and me. "These are their friends, Mark, Clark, David, Bradley, George, and Alex. There is another one, named John, but I think his mom is still sick," she said as she pointed at them. Mark waved at them like a child as we sat there unprepared for this quick surprise. But they just gave us one look then turned back around to glare at Dan. But Dan just stood there, smiling at them calmly. Then one of their wives said, "So, Jessie, what's for dinner?"

Jessie glared at her brothers and said, "Oh, come on in the kitchen and I'll show you." She started to walk into the kitchen, and we all followed her into the kitchen to eat.

While Jessie and her brothers' wives and kids sat in the kitchen talking, her brothers sat in the living room with us. There was this horrifying silence. Everyone just sat there, looking at each other eating. Till David quietly said, "Okay, is anyone going to say anything, 'cause I'm getting tired of all this silence." But no one said anything; they just sat there and stared at him.

"Thank you, Jessie," Alex said, swallowing Jessie's delicious food.

"You're welcome, Alex," Jessie said with a bright smile on her face.

"Yeah, thanks, Jess. You know one day you're going to have to teach me how to cook, because I have no clue when it comes to cooking," Mark said.

"Maybe one day," she said, getting up to go clean her dish, and the other woman handed her their dish, while one of them helped her. Which gave Jessie's brothers (besides Jason) a chance to start asking Dan a whole bunch of questions. Like, *What do you? How much do you love our sister? Who are your parents? Where do you live? When did you meet our sister?* It bugged me that they were asking Dan all these questions because some of these questions were personal questions. After a while, I could tell it was bugging the rest of us too. But Dan sat there, answering all their questions like a pro, smiling at them.

After a moment passed, Jason yelled, "Will you guys stop asking him all these questions. I mean, goodness sakes, give the guy a break, we just met him." As he walked into the kitchen, his voice started to fade.

Then Justin said, "We just want to know a little bit more…"

Then Jason just turned around. "Oh yeah, you're just trying to get to know him a little bit more, huh," he said as he glared at them.

"It's fine, Jason, I had a feeling that they were going to act this way once they saw me. I mean, you guys pretty much raised her since she was ten years old. So, I knew you guys would probably act overprotective like a dad," Dan said, walking over to Jason and into the kitchen.

"She told you that our parents are dead?" Joseph asked as he followed him to put his plate in the sink.

"Yeah, which me and my brothers know how that feels," Dan said as he pointed at us.

"What do you mean?" Justin asked.

"Well, our mom died half a year ago from cancer. But that's not as bad as losing both of your parents," he said as he walked out of the kitchen with Joseph behind him. Jason started to give his brothers funny looks. So Joshua asked, "Why are you giving us those looks?" but Jason just turned around and walked into the kitchen.

After dinner, Dan had to take Matt and me home, and the gang had to go to their homes too. So we said goodbye and left. When we got there, Dad was sitting on the couch, looking at the newspaper. "Where in the world did you boys go?" he asked, taking his glasses off.

"We were at Jessie's house," I said.

"Yeah, and we met her brothers too," Matt said.

"Oh really," Dad said, smiling at us.

"Yeah," Matt said, getting into the food.

"When do I get to, meet this girl of yours Dan?" he asked, sounding a bit upset.

"I don't know, you could meet her and her brothers at the park this weekend," Dan said.

"Okay, sounds good to me," Dad said as he walked into the kitchen to tell Matt to get out. Then I got in the shower. When I got out and dressed, Dan had already left. Dad and Matt were already going to sleep. So I finished reading *The Outsiders* and went to bed.

CHAPTER 8

It had been about two weeks since we met Jessie's brothers, and they were starting to like Dan now. It took Joshua a little longer to get used to Dan, but he liked him a lot more than he did at first. Their wives like him too. So do their kids; they like to call him Danny or Super Dan. Dan doesn't really mind. He just thinks it's funny that they call him Super Dan. But you can tell why they call him that. Because he kind of looks like Superman and is strong like Superman too. At least that's what the kids told me.

I thought it was clever that they say Super Dan instead of Superman. They like to call me Mickey and Matt, Mattey. We like that they call us that. It made Matt want Jessie and Dan to have kids. Jessie told him, "We're probably going to after we get married. Which will be in a few years or so." At that moment though, Matt seemed to have forgotten that Dan might not be able to have kids. He went to three different doctors, and they all told him the same thing: "There's a 25 percent chance that you'll be able to have kids." The sad part about this is that he was sixteen when he was told. Which is the real reason why he didn't have a girlfriend before Jessie. He was scared that if he told them that they would leave him like his high school sweetheart, Becky. Dan loved her more than any girl in the world. But when he told her he might not be able to have kids, she ignored him for weeks. Till he finally met up with her to talk. It didn't work out, but with Jessie it did. She told him that she would take that 25 percent chance because she loved him and that if they weren't able to make kids, they would adopt kids and make them the happiest kids in the world because having a happy and healthy kid was all she wanted. Which made Dan overwhelmed with joy.

Maybe that's why Dan and Jess have been getting a little bit more, let's just say, intimate. Like one time we caught them making out on the couch. It was very uncomfortable because Dan had his shirt off and was working on getting Jessie off. Although I was our fault for not knocking on the door. But we're used to not knocking on each other's homes. Especially Dan's house. He never used to have girl in his house. But that wasn't the last time we caught them. One time we went to Jessie's house because we knew Dan was there. The one thing about Jessie's house, though, is that her front door has a glass window in the middle of it that goes to the top and bottom of the door. And if you look through it, you can see most of the living room and about a quarter of the kitchen. Dan and Jess were in that little quarter of the kitchen. Jessie was on the counter, while Dan was standing up with Jessie's arms and legs wrapped around him. But we weren't the only ones who could see through it. Jessie saw us because the counter she was on was facing us. She told us that she warned Dan that we were there, but he didn't care till she threatened to kick him where it hurts the most, then he backed off and opened the door for us.

The thing that wasn't good these last few weeks was that John's mom passed away on May twenty-fourth, on a Thursday, year of 1984 because she had lung cancer from smoking. Her funeral is Wednesday next week.

When she was about twenty-one, she found out she was having John. She stopped smoking until she gave birth to him. And a few weeks after he was born, she started to smoke again. John had no idea that she had lung cancer. Although he knew she smoked. And to be honest, I think she knew that she had it but didn't want to worry John. So she kept it a secret from him. But she was a nice woman. She would always have something nice to say to you and always give you some advice if you were having problems or if you asked for some advice.

We all felt bad for John. He lost his only true love and now his only parent. His dad left him and his mother when he was still in her belly. When he called us and told us that his mom died, you could hear him crying and sobbing. Which usually he doesn't do and is something you would never think he would do because he's usually the big, mean, tough guy you see walking on the streets looking like he's up to no good. That's the kind of man John looks. But to hear him crying on the telephone makes him seem puny like instead of big and strong.

When Jessie heard that his mom passed away, she was heartbroken. We all were heartbroken. Some of us knew how it felt to lose your parent or parents. But we didn't know how it feels to lose your only parent who loved you dearly. When we went to go visit him, we realized that he'd been drinking, which he rarely did, unlike Bradley and Mark. There were beers and whisky bottles all over. They were on the floor, the table, and even in the bathroom. We saw him passed out on the couch. Dan started to shake him lightly then started to shake him harder and harder. Probably because he was thinking John was dead or something and got worried.

But he finally woke up and started to cry when he saw us. Then he asked Dan, "Why did she have to leave, Dan, why?" But Dan just sat there, trying to find something to keep him calm. After a while, Dan finally said, "I don't know, John. But I do know you can't start drinking because she left."

John yelled, "Why not, Dan?" He glared at him.

Dan yelled back, "Because she probably wouldn't want to see you living this way, John!" Dan crouched beside him, putting his hand on John's shoulder. John looked at him and nodded. Then he sat up, cupping his hands to his face and sliding his hands through his hair, and stood up and said, "You're right, Dan."

Dan smiled and said, "Yeah, I know. Now let's get you cleaned up."

John stopped drinking for a little while. Then started to drink again. It was like he was addicted to drinking now and was going to drink himself to death, and we knew we couldn't make him stop. So we decided to let him stop on his own.

But that wasn't the only bad thing that happened this week. Alex got jumped a few nights ago walking home from the movie house and got badly hurt too. He had a big cut on his face that had eleven stitches in it, a broken nose, and almost all his ribs were cracked. When Jessie and I visited him, she started to cry and blame herself because she was the one who dropped him off there. Sitting there, looking at my torn-up best friend made me cry and ask myself, why? Why would anyone want to do this to a kid who was just trying to get somewhere? Then Alex said in a soft voice, "It's not your fault, Jess. I was the one who decided to walk home alone in the dark." He moaned at the last word he spoke. She sat there, wiping her big crystal-clear tears from her soft, sweet cheeks, whimpering at his side like a puppy. Then I realized she was even beautiful when she cried, and I think Alex noticed it too, 'cause he started to smile.

When Alex's parents walked in, his mom started to sob then ran beside him and said, "Ohh, my poor baby, look what they did to you." she brushed his head with her small hand. Alex's parents already knew Jessie since she started to pick him up from school and drop him off at their house. They always tried to give her money for picking him up and dropping him off. But she just said she didn't need their money because she already had enough of it. But if I was her, I would've taken it and used it to get a new pair of sneakers, 'cause my sneakers were trash.

They're all ripped and taped up and have holes in them, where rocks and stuff get in them. But that's me, not her. She's too sweet and too kind to be greedy like I am. But I might be greedy because I'm young and young not-so rich people will take everything that's given to them as long as it's free. But rich kids are the whole opposite of us not-so-rich kids. They'll still take the money if it's given to them. But if it's something else, they'll just say, "We can just buy a new one of those at the store." They say this because they don't want to buy something that someone had already used, or they really can just buy it at the store for about 0.50 or more.

After we left the hospital, Jessie asked if I wanted to go to her house. I said no, although I really wanted to go to her house. The reasons I didn't want to go to her house were, one, I wasn't feeling good, and two, I was sad and angry that my best friend got beat up by those stupid rich kids that think they can jump us because we're poorer than they are, and they think it's fun. To me it's stupid that they think it's right for them to jump us all because we live differently from them. But I think we'll get even with those rich kids now that Alex got jumped by them.

When I got home, no one was there. So I made myself an egg sandwich that has lettuce, bacon, sausage, mayonnaise, mustard, and eggs in it. Then sat on the couch, turned on the television, and started to watch *The Cosby Show. The Cosby Show* is about an obstetrician, Cliff; his lawyer wife, Claire; their daughters, Sondra, Denise, Vanessa, and Rudy; and son, Theo. Based on the stand-up comedy of Bill Cosby, the show focused on his observations of family life. Although based on comedy, the series also addresses some more serious topics, such as learning disabilities and teen pregnancy. It isn't my favorite, but it's still something to watch. It was mom's favorite show. So was *Who's the Boss*.

My favorite show is *M*A*S*H**, which is about members of the 4077th Mobile Army Surgical Hospital care for the injured during the Korean War and use humor to escape from the horror and depression of the situation. Among the 4077's people are Captains Benjamin "Hawkeye" Pierce and Trapper John McIntire, Majors Margaret "Hot Lips" Houlihan and Frank Burns, and Corporal. Walter "Radar" O'Reilly. My second favorite is *Who's the Boss*, which is about a widower and former pro baseball player, Tony Micelli, who takes a job as a housekeeper for a high-powered divorced businesswoman, Angela Bower, and her son. He and his daughter, Samantha, move into the Bower residence, where Tony's laid-back personality contrasts with Angela's type-A behavior. Angela's man-hungry mother, Mona, is also in the mix.

Mom used to watch it every morning and would watch *The Cosby Show* in the afternoon and at night sometimes, and if I couldn't go to sleep, she would let me watch television with her. But she wouldn't have the television all the way turned up like Dad does. So that's not why I couldn't go to sleep. I couldn't go to sleep because my mind was always on at night. I wouldn't be thinking of anything; my mind just wouldn't ever rest. In the summer, Dad watches television all night long. But he at least turns it down when you ask him to.

And he doesn't watch television on school nights. Which is a good thing because if Dad is watching something that is pretty interesting, I would want to listen to it. Dad watches war movies and shows that teach you how to fix cars, and some teach you how to survive in the wilderness.

After I was done eating and done watching television, I washed my dishes then grabbed my book and started to read. Then my mind started to fade away from the world and into my imagination. I was still reading *The Outsiders*. I was now on the last chapter of it too. I really like this book. It's kind of like my life a little bit. The only part that isn't like my life is that my life isn't that terrible. Because I at least got one parent, and two of our gang members hasn't died yet. I started to think, what would my life be like if my dad died with my mom and Dan had to take care of me and Matt? It would probably be like the book almost, except it's in the eighties and not too harsh, but it could be terrible too. Dan would be mean to me, like Darry is to Ponyboy, and Matt would probably stick up for me, like Soda does, and they'll have to work every single day so I could get through school. Then I thought, what if it does happen? What if dad gets in a car crash and John kills himself because he can't take living without his mom and his girlfriend Marcie. The one person that will probably be fine is Alex because his injuries aren't that bad. So he'll get out of the hospital the day before John's mom's funeral. I finally got tired of reading it, so I just put it on my bed.

When I walked into the living room, George walked in with Bradley, Mark, David, and Matt.

"Hey, Mike, what are you going to do today?" Matt asked with some compassion.

"Nothing much, why, do you want me to go somewhere with you?"

Matt looked at all of us with a sad look then said, "Yeah, John wanted us to go to his house for something. But I think he was probably drunk at the time he called us and said that. But we're still going to go just in case it's important or something bad happened." He walked over to me, as I sat down to slip my shoes on.

After that, we all ran out the door and started to walk to John's house. Our house isn't that far apart. They're only three or four blocks apart from each other. Which is kind of nice because if we are having a problem or something, we can just go to each other's houses and stay there for a while. Like when Bradley got in trouble with the cops.

We all hid him until the cops gave up. Or if one of us is having problems with our parents, we go to someone's house and stay there till they make up. Once we were about two more blocks away from his house, I got a funny feeling. Like there were butterflies in my stomach. When I get this feeling, it usually means that something bad is about to happen, or I'm scared, or I like a girl. This rarely happens to me, 'cause I'm not into girls yet although I'm almost fifteen years old, and you would probably think it's not true that I don't like girls. I'm quite offended. Matt said I will sooner or later. But I want to wait till I'm out of school or when I'm at least seventeen or older, 'cause I want to focus on school right now.

Once we reached his house, we stopped at the edge of his house and examined it. We looked at each other like we didn't know what to do next. Then we finally walked up the steps. Matt knocked on the door, but there was no answer. So Matt just cracked the door open and peeked in and said, "Hello, John, are you in there?" We all walked in one at a time and looked around to see beer bottles everywhere. They were broken all through his house. It was also trashed too. The furniture was knocked over, everything that was on the court or in the cupboards was now on the floor all through the kitchen, the living room, into the hallway.

It seriously looked like a tornado went through it. The only thing that wasn't distorted was his telephone. "Man, it really stinks in here," George said, crinkling up his nose.

David chuckled then said, "No dur, George, I mean, look at all these beer bottles." He waved his hands out in front of him. After a few minutes of being there, we heard something fall and someone yell, "Son of a—!"

Matt ran toward the door where the noise was coming from, and we followed him. When we got there, it was locked. Matt tried to talk John into opening the door, but it wasn't working, so he tried knocking the door down. "Hold on, I got an idea," Mark said, and Matt stopped to listen. But we just watched Mark run to the end of the hallway and start to run toward the door as fast as he could. When he ran into the door, you could hear the cracking of the wood, see the doorknob popping out from the door. Then the whole doorknob flew off the door and hit Bradley straight in the forehead, making a big gash right in the middle, and the door was thrown open. John was sitting on the bed, crinkling up his face, getting ready to pull the trigger of an ALFA Combat. But then Matt ran and jumped on him. John fell down, and the ALFA Combat shot out a bolt, and it hit Matt on the side of the cheek, leaving a cut, and went through the ceiling.

The blood from the cut on Matt's cheek dripped onto John's white T-shirt, as Matt shook him as he started to cuss at him, calling him every name in the book. Mark grabbed the ALFA Combat out of John's hand before he could hurt someone and unloaded it then put it on the dresser next to him.

We were all surrounding John, while Matt was still shaking him and cursing at him with every dirty word he could think of. Bradley finally said, "That's enough, Matt. Now come on, give him a break." He put his hand on Matt's shoulder and the other on his head, where the cut was. I could see blood run between his fingers then drip onto the carpet once it got to the tip of his elbow.

Matt took a deep breath, trying to stay calm, as he let go of John's T-shirt then said, "Why were you about to kill yourself, John?"

"Because I'm tired of living this life of pain. Everyone leaves me. First my dad leaves me, then Marcie leaves, now my mom, and you know it's probably my fault that Alex got mugged last night," John said as he started to cry. You know there's nothing like watching a grown man cry like a big baby. My Uncle Tom told me when a man cries like that, it means he's hurt really bad. So I wasn't going to judge him.

"What do you mean it's your fault that Alex got mugged?" David asked as Matt got off him.

"I mean, he wanted me to go to the movie house with him. But I said no. If I went with him, he would've never got hurt. I could have protected him." Then it hit me: John didn't just start drinking on his own.

It was because he found out that Alex got hurt. "But instead, I decided to just let him get hurt. So it's my fault that he got jumped, all mine," he said as he covered his face with his hands and cried even more. Then George walked over to him and said, "John, it's not your—"

Then John yelled, "Yes, it is, George! You just don't know because you haven't had a screwed up life like I have!" He uncovered his face. George backed up a little bit when John said that. None of us had ever yelled at George or at each other before. So this was new to us all.

I guess John realized that he scared George and probably got a feeling that we were getting mad at him, especially Matt, because he started to look at all of us. "I'm sorry, kid, it's just that I've been through a lot my whole life, of people that I love leaving me."

"Yeah, we know, but that doesn't mean you should lock yourself in your room and kill yourself and scare the hell out of us," Matt said, still furious with him.

"Why not, Matt, why shouldn't I? My life is freaking hell anyways," John said, getting in Matt's face.

Then Matt yelled, "Because you're part of our family, John! So if you kill yourself, all of our lives will be a living hell and screwed up like yours is, John. At least that's what you say. But you know what, we've been there for you, John." He started to pace. "But you mostly been there for us. So if you want to kill yourself, go ahead and make our lives miserable. But I just want you to know we're not going to leave you, so don't think about leaving us." He swung his arms around.

This was the first time I'd ever seen Matt get mad. Usually he's a fun, goofy teenage street kid that winks at all the cute girls. To which they usually giggled or rolled their eyes or smile at him.

John sat down, probably surprised that he didn't think of how killing himself would affect us. "Whoa, I never thought about that.

I should've though. But I guess I was too busy drinking and going crazy. To you guys I probably looked like I lost it, huh."

Mark laughed and said, "Ohh yeah, you sure went crazy all right." The room seemed to have a bit more joy in it, 'til John began to frown.

"What's wrong, John?" Bradley asked with a puzzled look.

"Oh, it's just that I probably lost my job because I haven't been going there for a few days. Neither have I called them or anything," he said, rubbing his face.

"Oh, well, that's not good, not at all, John," George said.

"Yeah, I know. I'm going to have to call them and tell them why I haven't been going to work and why I didn't call them and tell them," John said, getting up off his bed and starting to walk into the hallway and into the living room.

We all followed him till he got to the telephone that was in the kitchen. Me and George started to look around then looked at John. John gave us a look then said, with a grumpy tone to his voice, "I know I need to clean my house, boys, so stop giving me those looks."

When someone answered and John told them why he hadn't been going to work and why he hadn't called in to work, then they started to talk about something else. And man, their conversation went on and on and on for hours it seemed like. I don't really know what they were talking about though. All I heard was the person on the other line saying, "You know boss is going to be ticked off at you, right."

John sighed and said, "Yeah, I know he is."

Once they were done talking, we started to clean up John's house. Me, David, and John cleaned up the living room. Matt, Mark, and Clark were cleaning up John's room. While Bradley and George cleaned his kitchen. When we were about halfway done with his house, David said, "You should go see Alex. It would probably make him feel better."

"No, David, I shouldn't, not like this," John said in grief.

That was when Matt explained, as he and Mark came out from the hallway and into the living room, "He's right, Dave, Alex would probably get worried about John, seeing him like this."

"Or he might be happy to see that he is doing better," David said, egging it on.

Matt sighed and said, "Maybe, maybe not, David, but if John doesn't want to go, then he doesn't have to, okay." David rolled his eyes and started to clean and mumble his complaints, but we ignored him.

No one said anything to anyone. Which made it quite all through John's house. Until sirens went off down the street. The sirens were either the ambulance or the police coming to John's house because someone heard the gunshot. My guess was that it was the police.

George and I looked out the window to find two police cars running down the street and parking by John's house. Two cops stepped out of each car and started to walk toward John's stairs.

"Well, that's not good," George said.

"What's not good, George?" Bradley asked as he went to look out the window. But before he could look, the police knocked on the door. We all looked straight at the door, then looked at John, and John looked at us. David then murmured "Well" as he did a quick shrug.

"I know, David," John said angrily.

We walked toward the door. When his hand reached out to grab the doorknob, I got chills all through my body, like it got cold all of a sudden. I didn't know why I got so cold. I think it might be because I had a feeling that something bad was about to happen or something like that. Once John opened the door, my heart stopped. It stopped so fast and for so long that I was feeling a little dizzy. That was when I realized I was obviously afraid of cops. Once the door opened, one of the cops said, "Hey, John, how are you today?" I sighed in relief once I heard the officer's voice. I could tell that it was our uncle Robert.

Robert is on our mom's side of the family. He's four years younger than her. We don't really see him much because he's a cop and has a family to take care of, but they don't even see him much either. The only time they do is on the weekends and sometimes on Wednesday. His wife, Sherry, worries about him. I can see why, because he usually is trying to arrest murderers, robbers, kidnappers, and drug addicts.

Our mom also has an older sister named Brooke, who's a librarian at the public library in town. Robert is always making sure we don't get into trouble. Even me, George, and Alex. Which we don't get in a lot of trouble. But that's if no one tries to harm any one of us. We'll fight rich kids in the halls or in class if they're disturbing one of us. Especially when they're teasing George. Because he's younger than the rest of us and pretty much a little brother to all of us.

"I've been better," John said, rubbing the back of his neck. Usually when he does this, it either means he's worried or he's thinking really hard.

"Someone called us about a gunshot at your house, so we came down here to make sure everything was all right," he said looking at us, and John stopped rubbing his neck to look at us too.

"But don't worry, we're not going to arrest you, because everyone looks okay. Except black and blue," Robert said, pointing at Bradley, whose cut had started to get bruised around it. "So you can calm down, John."

John's smile revealed itself in relief. I walked over behind John and said, "Hey, Uncle Robert."

Robert walked up to where I was standing and said, "Well, hey there, little buddy, how ya doing?" He put his elbow on my shoulder. I smiled as I folded my arms and said, "Just fine, until you came here," in a sarcastic way.

He cocked one eyebrow and said, "Well, what in the hell of an attitude is that?" He wrapped the arm he had on my shoulder around my neck and rubbed my head. Then someone was trying tell them something on their radio. So our uncle Robert's partner stepped into the car to copy back to them and said, "There's a fight going on at the park, Officer Roberts." Robert stopped and walked down the stairs.

"Okay, tell them we're on our way there." He turned around and said, "I'm sorry, boys, I would stay longer, but…I gotta get back to work." He turned back around to hop inside the driver side of the police car. Matt squeezed between me and John and walked in front of us to say, "Well, can we come with you?" Our uncle Robert slammed his door then said no as he shook his head then drove off.

We stood there on the porch, watching them speed off, till Bradley said, with a slight smirk, "You know, we could just run to the park, right." We all looked at each other, grinning, and the next thing I know, we're sprinting to the park.

As we were running, I saw the police car that Robert jumped into and the other police car trailing behind him. Then I started to think we were running pretty fast. But then I realized they had to turn on corners, while we were running in a straight line.

Once we got there, the fight was between a big group of rich kids and Blake Frederick's gang. Man, let me tell you, they were really getting at it too. The biggest problem was that Blake's gang was getting banged up pretty good. So Matt, David, Mark, and Clark were gonna jump in and help. But John put his arms out in front of them to stop them and said "I got this" as he grinned at us. I saw Bradley put his head down and shake it back and forth. Then lift it back up and say, "The grizzly bear is going to come out of his cave, and he ain't happy neither." He was still shaking his head back and forth.

John took a few steps forward, puffed up his chest, and put his arms on his hip, and we copied behind him. But we folded our arms.

He took a deep breath and yelled "Hey!" as loud as he could, and they all froze in their fighting positions. "Listen, the cops are coming here. So you guys might want to scat," John said as Blake's gang and the big group of rich kids backed away from each other and listened to what John had to tell them.

One of the rich kids snottily said, "Why should we listen to you?"

Blake turned to him and said, "Probably so you guys don't get put into jail." He and the rich kid walked to each other.

"Oh no, they're going to put you in jail, you bum." the rich kid said as they were face-to-face.

"Who are you calling a bum, scumbag?" Blake said as his voice got deep.

"You!"

"Oh yeah?"

"Yea!"

Then Blake socked him in the face, and the fight was back on. "Oh come on, guys," John said in disappointment. Bradley than ran past him, shouting "Let's get it on!" as he jumped right in the middle of the fight. John signed and said, "If you guys want to join him, you can. I'm not going to stop you." Then he started to smirk. "Because I'm going to be in it too." He ran and tackled two high-class kids. Then Mark, David, Clark, and Matt folded him. George and I looked at each other as if confused.

"Should we?" George asked.

Then Bradley yelled, "Are you two going to fight with us or not?" Then he turned around and slugged a rich kid. George and I looked at each other one last time. I shrugged and said, "Oh, what the heck, why not." George smiled at me, and we ran right into the fight.

CHAPTER 9

Sitting there at the police station with George in the middle of me and Mark, who's by Clark and David on my right side. On my left side, there's John, sitting by Matt and Bradley, who were sitting on the ground. I knew for sure that Dad was going to be mad at Matt and me and maybe John too since he didn't stop us, and he's older than us. But probably mostly me, like usual. Now I know that Dad and I apologized to each other. But that isn't going to change anything or make anything better between us. 'Cause Dad is Dad, and I am Mike, and there's no changing the way we really feel about each other.

But anyways, I could still hear the sirens going off in my head, or maybe it was just outside the police station. I don't know. *Whatever, I'm tired and beat up,* I thought to myself. But those sirens must be from outside the station because they started to fade away after a little while.

Man, that fight was sure rough for just a sock fight. It might be because the rich kids had more members that kept coming and coming when they saw the fight, until Robert came with his police buddies, and they all scattered like rats off into their cars and drove off. I could still see the look on Robert's face when I closed my eyes, and it wasn't a happy look. It was a mad look with his arms folded and his eyes glaring down on us like the devil on David's arm without the creepy smile, though. Our uncle Robert usually doesn't get mad, kind of like Matt, but when he does get mad, you do not want to be around. He's almost as bad as Dad. But not as bad as Dad. Nobody is as bad as Dad. Then again, dad's been through a lot. But not as much as John. As you heard before, his dad ran off after he was born, he lost his girlfriend, and then his mom. He and his mom were very close, but he isn't alone. He still has the gang, and this gang is family. We might not have the same blood, but that doesn't make us family. Being there when we need each other the most is what makes us family. But I think John hasn't learned that yet.

When Robert came around the corner with Blake Fredrick, we all stared at them both. Till Blake glared down at us and growled, "What are you punks looking at?" Robert got him uncuffed. We all turned our heads away from him because we knew better then to look at Blake straight in the eyes. Because he can make your life a living hell. Like I said before, Blake is more than just mean. He looks mean too with this huge scars all over his body that he wears with pride. Which he got from blade fights in New York. After he got out of the hospital, he came to our town and made a gang. Ever since that, he's been going to jail every month, nonstop. For all the reasons of getting into jail. Like robbing stores, sometimes the rich kids, or he slashed their tires or steals their cars and drops them off somewhere and all kinds of stuff that I can't explain.

Blake's two years older than Dan. He's also the same height as him too. He has a dirty-strawberry blond hair with gray-green eyes that strikes fear right into your heart if you look into them for a long while. But there's a reason why Blake is the way he is nowadays. When he was younger, his dad used to beat him up when he got home, and his mom tried to stop it from happening, but then he would slap her till she bled. At least that's what Blake told me. He told me that when he saw a bunch of rich kids picking on me. I was eleven years old at the time and not as scared of him. He was walking me home, and he told me his whole childhood and told me not to tell anyone because that would ruin his reputation, and I didn't. The one thing I didn't expect him to say was that I shouldn't ever be like him because his life is a disaster even though he didn't act like it. I wasn't going to be like him anyways, and I never will.

When Robert uncuffed Blake, he said, "All right, boys, you're good to go. Now please stay out of trouble." He put cuffs in their place on his belt. "Okay," we all said besides Blake. He doesn't like cops. The only thing he likes about them is that they're rough with him and they're rougher with him when he teases them. So the more he teases them, the more rough they'll be with him.

Robert started to walk away then stopped and turned around to say, "Ohh, Matt, Mike, I called your dad and your big brother's girlfriend, Jessie, they both said they'll see if they can get off early."

"Okay, thanks, Uncle Robert."

"No problem, boys," he said as he turned around and walked off. Matt shook his head in his hands and said "Dad's going to be so mad at us" as he rubbed his face.

"It's okay, kid, I'll tell him what happened," John said, putting his arm around Matt.

I realized that something was wrong with Matt. He would never act this way at all. Probably even if our uncle Robert put him in jail. So why was he acting so scared of Dad? Dad wasn't going to yell at him. He was going to yell at me, unless Jessie got here before he does. Then maybe he won't go crazy on us. He'd probably be so happy to finally meet Jessie that he probably won't pay any attention to us.

We were sitting there for about twenty minutes, while Blake teased Bradley with his six-inch switchblade, but when a cop would walk by us, he would stop and hurry to put it away before they saw it. Anyways, we finally heard the police door slam and someone marching toward us like a bull on a rampage. That's how you know it's our dad. When he's mad at least. But then again, when he's sad, stressed out, disappointed, or scared, he's still mad as a bull. The only time he isn't mad is when he's happy. Which he barely is. The only time he is, is when Matt makes him laugh. Well, chuckle, more like. Or if Matt has a new girlfriend and is showing her to him. Which it seems to me that he always has a new one every month or so. But it's not his fault; it's their fault. They only like him because he's good-looking, not for who he is or for his personality.

They always seem to break his heart. But he doesn't cry about it like he used to. The first girls to break his heart he cried for days over. After the fifth or sixth girl broke his heart, he started to ask, "Why doesn't any girl like me for who I am?" I felt bad for him, and I still do too. But the one thing I think he needs to learn is that he won't find the perfect girl right now. But when he does find the right girl, I hope she loves him for who he is and not just because he's handsome.

As we sat there watching Dad march over to us, Blake started to tease us when he said, "Ooh, here comes big daddy to come and kick some ass..." We started to look at him. "And how I can't wait to see some of that action happen." He walked to the other bench across from us and sat down and sat his head on his hand as he smirked at us. John glared at him and shook his head then turned to see Dad standing in front of us, glaring down at all of us.

John sighed as he stood up. "Mr. D, it's—"

Before he could say much more, Dad yelled, "Sit your ass back down, young man!" He pointed at the bench. It didn't take long for John to sit back down. Probably because he knew better then to tick Dad off and to talk back to him. For one good reason. One day John was smack talking and being a smart ass to everyone, including Dad, and the rest of our parents. So Dad knocked him down and put him in a headlock and started to tell him that he'll do worse than put him in a headlock. But that's not all he said. He also had the "grow up" talk with him. Which is where Dad yells in your ear about being a man and how much harder life is when you're an adult. After that, John never talked back to anyone.

But anyways, Dad kept yelling at us with paranoid and angry words spilling out of his mouth, as Blake laughed his heart out behind him. Till Dad turned around and yelled at him, "You shut your trap, boy, or else it will be more than words coming out of my mouth." Then he turned back around and said, "Now where were we." He stopped to think. "Oh, that's right, wondering why in the hell you think it's a good idea to get into a fight when you knew police were going over to stop it." He folded his arms at us.

Before anyone could answer, we heard a girl yell "Boys!" in a distressed-like voice. We all looked to see Jessie standing in the sunshine that shone through the glass doors. Man, she looked beautiful like that, with the sun making her hair a golden dusk color. When George saw her, he made a confused look and said "Jessie?" as he tilted his head to one side. Once she started to jog over to us, I saw why he was so confused. She was wearing her black-and-white sneakers, with shorts, a white tank top tucked in them, a red plated T-shirt over it tied at the bottom, and a baseball cap.

Once she got to us, she started examining mine and George's faces. She made a pouty face and said "Oh, why did you guys have to get in that fight?" as she rubbed our cheeks. Then she stood up and folded her arms, waiting for an answer. But we just sat there, not knowing what to tell her.

Dad looked at us then at her and asked, still sounding a little mad, "Now who are you?"

Jessie looked at him and said, "Oh, I'm Dan's girl—"

That's when Dad interrupted her, looking like his eyes were about to pop out. "You're Dan's girlfriend!" he said as if amazed that Dan actually found a girl.

Jessie just smiled and said, "Yes, I am," still folding her arms.

Dad froze up for a few seconds then said, "Oh my goodness, Dan said you were gorgeous, but I didn't believe him." He grinned at her. And let me tell you, I've never seen dad so happy since mom died. I mean, he's happy to see Matt bring a girl into the house. But not as happy as he is right now. Behind Dad, Blake sat there with his mouth wide open as he started to slowly slouch down, scanning Jessie up and down. It seemed to me that he'd never seen a girl like Jessie before.

After sitting there for about ten seconds, he finally walked over to Jessie and said, "So you're Dan's girl, huh." He said it with that bad look in his eyes.

Jessie gave him a funny look and said, "Yeah," facing toward him.

Blake smirked at her and said, "Then remind me not to hit on you so I don't get my head knocked in by him." He started to walk off. Once he closed the door, Jessie looked at us all confused with her mouth cracked open. But nothing came out.

Dad smiled at her and said, "That's Blake. He said that because Dan kicked his butt one time because he wouldn't stop teasing him."

"Why would Dan do that? He doesn't seem like he would do that," Jessie said, giving Dad a weird look.

"Well, that's because he was a teenager when he kicked Blake's butt," Dad said, explaining, "but he probably won't be doing that since he's with you now. So don't worry about it."

"Hey, Dad, are we still in trouble for—"

Before Matt could finish, Dad interpreted him and said, "Yes, Matt, you guys are still in trouble." Matt sighed. "Now let's go home so I can finish yelling at you guys," Dad said, smiling at us. Was he actually joking for once, I thought to myself. Dad never jokes around, never ever. It's probably because Jessie's here, and he didn't want to give a bad impression.

Jessie came to the house with us. She didn't drive her car to the police station. I asked her why, and she said, "It was a good day to go on a walk," shrugging. When we got home, Dad immediately started to cook dinner for us. Jessie helped him and started to give him some advice on his cooking. Dad didn't seem to mind that she was. But if any of us were to question his cooking, he'd probably tell us to "shut our mouths" and "eat what I give you." But it might be because she's a girl, a sweet and gorgeous girl in fact. Not only that, she was Dan's sweet, gorgeous girl.

When Jessie got done giving Dad advice and Dad got done cooking, Dan walked right in through the door. When he saw Jessie, he smiled and said, "There you are. I was wondering where you were, little woman." He shut the door behind him.

"I asked your brothers where you were, they told me that you went to the police station to go see Mikey and the rest of the guys," he said, walking up to her. "So I drove all the way there, and guess what?" he said as if disappointed.

Jessie folded her arms and said, "What?"

Dan leaned forward and whispered, "You weren't there." He leaned back up and shrugged. We all started to chuckle at him. But Jessie shook her head at him, trying not to laugh.

"I'm so sorry, Dan." She giggled.

"It's okay, it's not your fault," he said, rubbing her cheek. He looked at us. Then back at Jessie. We knew what he was going to say when we saw that smirk on his face. "It was those knuckleheads' fault." He thumbed us and looked back at us. "They're the ones who didn't think before they jumped into conflict at the park when Robert told them not to." Then he started to walk over to us. He looked at John.

John knew what was coming and said, "Don't start, Dan, I'll kick you in the behind," in a playful way.

Dan cocked an eyebrow and said, "Oh, really, Johnny boy." They acted like they were going to wrestle around.

"Yeah, let's get him, Dan," Matt said as he and Mark jumped beside Dan. Then Bradley and Clark jumped on John's side.

"Let's take them down, Johnny," Bradley said as he put his fist up.

Then David jumped in the middle and said, "There isn't just two parties, there's three."

Dad started to laugh at us, and Jessie rolled her eyes at us like we were retarded. "I think y'all knuckleheads." She folded her arms and leaned against the sofa.

Dan gave her a sarcastic glare and said, "What did you just say, woman?" He walked over to her very slowly with us walking behind him, grinning happily.

"Oh, I think you heard me, Danny," she whispered squint at him. Dan leaned forward.

"Oh, did I. I thought I didn't listen very well." He put his hands on the sofa. "Because you know that I don't have good ears." He started to smirk at her.

Jessie rolled her eyes once more and said "Here we go again" very quietly.

Dan gave her a funny look again and said, "What was that, did you say something woman? 'Cause I swear I saw your mouth move. But I'm not sure." He started to squint back at her.

She started to hide her giggles as she said, "You're not funny, Danny," as she leaned forward to him.

"If I'm not funny, then why are you laughing?" He started to glared at her as if suspicious.

She put her finger on his chest and said, "Because you're acting stupid," as she backed him up. But before she started to walk away, he wrapped his arms around her waist and pulled her in and started to tickle her and kiss her everywhere on her face. "Dan, stop it," Jessie said, trying to get away from him. We sat there, not knowing what to do and now not smiling, looking at them awkwardly. At least my point of view. Don't get me wrong. It was cuter than hell. They were just being too sexual.

Then Dad walked out of the kitchen and said, "Daniel, stop it. None of us want to see you showing affection." He put his hand on Dan's shoulder. Dan looked at him and paused. Dad looked at us to explain, "And not only that, but dinner's done too." He thumbed toward the kitchen.

Dan looked at us as his cheeks started to blush. "Oh, I'm sorry, guys." He let go of Jessie. She gave him a nasty look. Dan sighed and said, "Oh, but mostly sorry for you, my little, pretty woman." He kissed her forehead. She wrinkled her nose a little.

"Are you ever going to stop kissing me?" she asked, smirking at him. He smiled at her and kissed her nose and said no like a child.

After we were done eating, Dan took Jessie home, and George and Bradley then left ten minutes after they did. Me and Matt had to clean the dishes after they all left the house. While dad sat on the couch, looking at the newspaper, he started to smile. "I like her, she's sweet." But Matt and I just kept cleaning dishes till he said, "She kind of reminds me of your mother." He looked at us then looked back at the newspaper. "Sweet, funny, with a little bit of sass," he said. But Matt and I didn't say anything thing to him. "If it wasn't too early, I would say she's the one for him"—as he folded the newspaper—"so he might as well keep her 'cause let me tell you, he'll never find another girl like her." He got up and threw away the newspaper. "Hey, boys, let me finish the dishes so you can get ready for bed. It's been a long day." He put a hand on each of our shoulders.

"Okay, Dad," Matt said.

"Good night, Dad," I said.

As we walked away, I heard Dad say, "One down, two more to go," as he started to do the dishes.

Chapter 10

It had been about a half month after the fight and since Dad met Jessie. It had also been about week since John's mom's funeral, and one thing I found funny about it is that John didn't shed one tear, even when he had to talk about his mom. But that doesn't mean he didn't care. During his last paragraph, John explained, "I promised my mother I wouldn't cry when this day came so she wouldn't have to listen to me whimper over her grave like a lost puppy. At first I wasn't sure if I would be able to keep it, but it's a promise to a family member, and promises given to family are the promises that should come first and the ones that are most important out of anyone you know because those are the people who never let you stand alone and been there when you need them the most. And my mom has been there since my dad left, when I lost Marcie, even when I was a stubborn teen. She stayed because she loved me, and she knew I needed her as much as she need me, so she stayed till she had no choice." John took a long sigh before saying, "But I'm not alone, thanks to these boys who helped me realize that they are just as much as family as my mom was to me. They've been there, and because of them, I'm still here. If I never met them, you guys would've buried two people today. I'm proud to call them my brothers." After he said that, we ran up to him bawling our eyes out to give him a big bear hug.

When I woke up the next day, no one was at the house. I looked in Dad's room then Matt's room. They weren't in there. At least that's what I thought. I mean, Dad wasn't there, Matt wasn't there, the gang wasn't there, and for once, it was actually quiet. So quiet without the radio or television on.

Until I walked in the kitchen and found Blake standing right next to the entrance, waiting to say, "Hey, kiddo." I jumped back. Not just because I didn't know he was there, but because of his voice. Blake has a very deep voice that gives you chills up and down your spine. "How ya doing?" he asked before taking a big bite of an egg salad sandwich.

"Gosh, dang it, Blake, you scared the jeepers out of me," I said as I walked into the kitchen. He chuckled.

"I'm sorry, kid," he replied as he swallowed and took more bites.

I took out the egg carton and took out two eggs from it so I could make some yolk eggs. "Where's my dad?" I asked as I cracked the first egg open.

He finished his sandwich then said, "Oh, he's at work." I cracked the second egg open onto the pan. "Yeah, he wanted me to babysit you." He licked his fingers. I turned to him.

"Yeah right, he wouldn't let you babysit me or anyone in fact," I snapped at him. He grinned at me.

"Yeah, you're right, I'm just too bad to babysit you," he said. I didn't say anything back to him. I just stared at him because I didn't know what to tell him. It was just that moment you sit there, knowing the person who can't help anyone with anything is telling you the real reason why they can't. "Well, I better get going," he said as he walked out of the kitchen. "Oh, and tell your big brother we're going to have a rumble with the high-class kids tomorrow night," he said, opening the door. I took a step out of the kitchen

"We're having a rumble tomorrow night?" I asked him with a curious look.

"Yep."

"Can I go?"

"Of course you can go, I'm not gonna stop ya. The more the merrier."

I smiled. "Okay, bye, Blake." I stepped back into the kitchen.

"Bye, little man." He started to walk out the door. Then I walked out of the kitchen to ask why, but he was already out the door by then. It might be because Alex got jumped, and they never finished the fighting at the park, I thought to myself. Then thought maybe I should go see how good ole Alex was doing as I flipped my eggs.

After I ate my eggs and cleaned my plate, I started to walk to Alex's house, which isn't that far away from ours. When me and Alex were younger, we used to meet right between our house, then go to George's house and pick him up, because he was younger than us, and his parents didn't want him walking alone on the street. Because during our golden years, there was a kidnapper in town, so we made a plan to go see each other. Alex and I would meet up first 'cause we were older and more responsible, at least that's what our parents told us.

Then we would go and pick up George at his house and go anywhere besides uptown, or else we would get a good whooping and wouldn't be able to see each other for a whole week. So we stand as far away from town as possible. But we don't do that anymore since there aren't any kidnappers, and now we're old enough to walk alone. Except in town, where all the high-class kids are that will track us down with their cars, then tease us, and mug us when we're just trying to get to our neck of the woods. Which, where we live, isn't the peachiest place ever. But it's home to us low-class kids and the only place we'll ever call home probably.

Once I got to Alex's house, I knocked and knocked on the door. But no one answered, so I walked down their steps, thinking they might not be there, till the door opened, and Alex's mom popped out behind it. She smiled at me. "Hi, Mikey," she said as she opened the door more. I smiled back up at her.

"Hi, is Alex here?" I asked as I put my foot on the first step.

"Oh yes, he's—"

Then before she could say anything else, Alex popped out between her and the doorway with a big grin on his face. "Hey, Mike, how are you?" he asked as he walked down the steps and gave me a big hug as if he hadn't seen me in years.

I hugged him back gently and said, "I was going to ask you the same thing." I started to grin. He let go.

"Pretty good for getting a big cut on my face plus a broken nose and both of my ribs being cracked," he said as he patted me on the shoulder. Alex looked up at his mom. "Right, Mom?" He smiled happily at her. But she just rolled her eyes.

"Okay, you two, are you going to come inside or what?" She put her hands on her hips.

We walked inside and into Alex's room as Alex began to say, "First things first." He jumped on his bed. "How's the gang, what's going on, are there any problems, oh, and are Jess and Dan still together?" As he sat up straight on the end of his bed, I sat there, thinking about what had happened and what was going on. I finally thought it through.

"Well, the gang's doing fine. There's going to be a rumble tomorrow night, and—"

That's when Alex interrupted me. "There's going to be a rumble?" His eyes widened.

"Yep."

"Ah, man, I wish I could go." He slouched down on his bed even more. "But my mom probably won't let me, you know how she is."

"Yeah, I know," I said as I sat down beside him.

Then I began to tell him what happened since he was in the hospital. As I explained to him, I realized that he seemed to be happy. But why would he be happy that all this was happening? I guess that's how my best buddy is, happy all the time. No matter what happens to him. But once he heard about John drinking, that smile of his started to fade away. At the end of the story, he seemed to be mad at John. John is like a big brother to Alex and David. They don't have any siblings, so they pretty much call each other brothers. I mean, Alex might be a big brother to a baby boy or girl. He told me he wanted it to be a girl. So his mom could do her hair and all kinds of girly stuff and just because he wants a little sister. Ever since he was ten, he'd always wanted a little sister. I asked him why, but he just shrugged at me.

I sat there listening to Alex's anger and frustration as he dug for a T-shirt in a basket, but to be honest, I wasn't really listening to what he was saying. Now I know that's bad, but I was tired. The only thing I heard him say was "Why does John have to be so stupid?" as he took off his T-shirt. "I mean, I get that he would start drinking when his mom died. But to start drinking when I get hurt, no." After he put on his shirt and turned to look at me, I looked at him for a few seconds.

Then I said, "Well, you do look really badly hurt, but I guess if it doesn't hurt you, then yeah." But he did look terrible, and I mean terrible. His nose was bruised, he had a black eye, and that cut on his face reminded me of Blake Frederick's scars that went across his eye, and his ribs were wrapped up. I felt bad for Alex but also felt bad for John. Alex shouldn't be mad at him. John was in a bad place before Alex got hurt. Besides him, David and Alex are like brothers. So of course, John is going to start drinking. John just feels like he's hurting everyone. His dad leaves him, his girlfriend dies in a car accident, his mom dies, and just to top it off, his little brother figure gets jumped by stupid high-class kids.

I don't understand why they really jump us. Like, do they do it for fun or because they want us to feel terrible about ourselves, like we already don't know that our life is sucky. Or maybe they think it's cool to chase a kid with their car and then ambush them when they're just trying to get somewhere. To me, it's unfair that they get away with everything, and we get the short end of the stick.

I finally got tired of him babbling about John. So I stood up and said, "It's not his fault that he feels like he's distressing everyone. It's not his fault that everyone he loves gets hurt or, worse, like dies. Neither is it your problem anyways!" I finally stopped to see Alex bug-eyeing me. "I'm sorry, Alex, it's just you shouldn't be so harsh with John. Besides, he's getting better now." I sat down. "Maybe you should go see him. Maybe that will make him feel a little better that you're not terribly hurt."

Alex sat there, still surprised that I yelled at him. Till he finally knocked himself out of it. "Yeah, sure, let's do that today," he said very slowly.

We walked out of his bedroom, and before we could walk out of the house, Alex's mom said, "Ah, Alexander Swindle, don't get in any trouble." She gave him a serious, motherly look. Alex gave her a crooked smirk.

"I know, don't worry."

He started to walk out the door, till his mom stopped him and said, "And if you see a Mustang following you, don't just try to keep it cool. Come home or to one of the boys' house before they—"

Before she finished, Alex said, trying to get outside the house, "I know, Mom, don't worry. This time I got somebody with me." His mom started to grip the washcloth that was in her hand, with her worried, sweet eyes staring at us like all mothers do to their kids when they're hurt. Alex took a short sigh and walked over to her. "Mom, I know you're worried about me, but I'll be fine." He took her hands and the washcloth with them. "Besides, we're going to John's house, okay, he won't let anyone hurt us." Alex knows how to talk his mom into doing things. He can talk any girl into things because he's the magic man. Like that one time our moms wouldn't let us go to a rumble, until he gave them a little talk, and they bought it and said we could go. I don't know how in the world he does it, but he can sure talk to girls. We don't know how he has this special power. At least that's what David said it was. No one knows how he got it. But one thing's for sure, he's good at it.

We were about halfway to John's house when Alex said, "I think my mom and dad are trying for a baby," with his hands stuffed in his pockets looking up at the sky. I looked at him.

"How do you know?"

He looked back at me with a smirk on his bruised face. "How do you think?" He cocked one eyebrow. I got a weird feeling in my stomach.

"Oh," I said, looking away from him. But he kept staring at me. I felt chills crawling up my back. "Ahh, uhh." I shivered. I hated to think of two people, well, you know. I just can't stand it. I just can't. I mean, I know that's how you make babies, but come on, I don't want to hear or talk about other people making babies. It's just nasty talking about other people doing it.

Alex started to die laughing. I just sat there with that weird feeling still in my stomach. I remember when Matt told me his first time. He was fifteen at the time. I don't know why he told me, his little brother who was only twelve, about it and how he did it. I don't ever want to hear him or anyone tell me about it and especially how they did it. At least Dan never told me. But I know he did it, because one night he never came home after football practice, and usually he was always there in a heartbeat. So Mom and Dad don't ask him a bunch of questions, like, "Where were you?" or "You better not be doing bad things." I asked Dad if he knew where he was, but he only said, "Losing his boyhood." At the time I didn't know what he meant by that, but now I for sure do. The next day I heard Dan in the bathroom. I knew it was him by his whistle. He always whistles "Crazy Love" when he's doing something or if he's taking a shower. So I jumped off my bed and ran to see if it was him. I threw the door wide open, and there was fifteen-year-old Dan with a towel wrapped around his waist and a toothbrush sticking out of his mouth. He jumped.

"Wow, little brother," he said as he was turning away from me. "What ya doing?"

I glared at him. "Where were you, Dan?" I took a few steps toward him. He sat there, looking around. Then Dad yelled, "Yeah, Danny boy, where in the hell were you, little man?" He looked up from his newspaper with a smirk on his face. Dad knew where he was. Dan smirked back at him.

"Um, I was…losing my…boyhood," he said, stumbling over his words, then turned away from me. I glared even more.

"I don't know what that means," I said then stomped off. Then stomped back and said, "I'm watching you." I gave him a steady pointing. I heard Dad laughing in the background.

Alex calmed down a little bit and asked, "Did your parents ever do it?"

I looked at him again. "Well, maybe, I don't know!" I shouted. "They never did it when I was around, or I never noticed." I shrugged.

Alex finally stopped laughing and said, "Yeah, I found out last night." He pointed toward town. I didn't say anything. I just kept walking. But I did start to think about what Dan and Jessie's kids might look like. I mean, Dan is big and strong, while Jessie is small and gorgeous. Not to say, but how many boys would they have till they had a girl? How would Dan react to it, would he be mad, sad, worried, or happy about having a little girl? Oh, whatever, I'll find out in the future.

I noticed Alex was still talking to me, not about how he found out that his parents were wanting to have a baby, but about what he wanted it to be. "I want the baby to be a little girl," he said with a joyful smile. I gave him a dreadful look.

"Why?"

He looked at me. "Well…" he started, "so I have a good reason to beat up boys and because I want a little sister around." He looked away from me. "It would be really nice." To me that didn't sound like a good reason why he wanted a little sister. Maybe he didn't know why he wanted a little sister, or maybe he just really wanted one.

When we got to John's house, Alex just walked in like he owned the place and yelled, "Oh, Johnny boy." He stopped right in the middle of the living room. "Guess who it is." He threw his arms out like he was going to give him a hug. I heard footsteps coming from the hall. Then John stepped out with a screwdriver in his hands and a dazed look.

"Alex?" His face started to change to an on-edge look. But Alex still had a big smile on his face.

"The one and only, buddy," he said with his arms still out.

John stood there, scanning him, then said, "What…what are you…umm…doing here?" He was now looking a little upset. Alex put his arms down and said, "I came here to see you." He took a few steps toward him, still having a joyful smile. John now had an angry and confused look on his face.

"Well, you shouldn't have." He started to walk away. Alex's smile started to fade away.

"Why not?" He was turning his head on one side. John looked at him.

"Because, Alex…" He turned back around, not knowing what else to say. Alex started to get angry with him.

"Because why?" He followed John through the hall. John kept walking.

"Just because," John said, starting to grip the screwdriver in his hand. I was trying to stop Alex. So I grabbed him by his shoulder and said, "Alex, just stop, he's not in a good mood." But Alex ripped my hand off his shoulder and started to walk over to John once again, who was trying to fix the door. Alex stopped next to him and started to yell out his fury.

"Just because I'm hurt, John, doesn't mean it's your fault, and just because someone dies doesn't—"

John didn't let him finish. He walked over to Alex, put his hands on his shoulders, and said, "You wanna know why I think it's my fault? Do you wanna know why I don't want you here?" He was shaking him with each question. Alex's face changed from mad to startled. I knew why. One, John is a lot, and I mean a lot, bigger than Alex; two, John has never ever shaken Alex before or even gotten mad at him. Like you heard before, they're like brothers. Mostly because they don't have siblings and they've pretty much known each other longer than I've known them.

John was still shaking Alex when he said, "It's because I hurt people, and I don't want to hurt you even more than I already have. You're like a little brother to me." Alex's lip started to tremble, and he hugged John. Once I heard one sniffle, I knew Alex was crying. John gave him one of his famous bear hugs, and I stood there awkwardly, not knowing what to do. Then I noticed John was crying too. So I stood there even more awkwardly. Till John said, "Come over here, ya knucklehead." He reached one arm out for me. I felt better that he wanted me to get into this sad but awkward moment. At least it was awkward to me.

After we helped John fix the doorknob, we had a long conversation about John's mom's funeral, Dan and Jessie, and the rumble. Then it got interrupted by Alex's mom, who was worried about him and told him to come home immediately. Of course Alex started to whine about how he was at John's house and that he was fine. But she started to yell into the telephone, and Alex had to hold it a foot away from his ear. Then John told her that he was fine and that he could stay or at least tried to, but she started to yell at John. So Alex and I had to go to his house. John walked us outside and stood on the porch.

Then we saw that flaming Mustang slowly coming toward us on the street. It was Chris and his friends. I could see that he at least had three or four friends with him. John walked down the steps, and we walked down them. His car pulled up right in front of us, and the sun reflected on the car, and the ray of sunlight shot me in the eyes. I was blind for a few seconds then got used to the brightness. Once they all stepped out, John asked, "What do you guys want?" He gave them a good glare.

Chris smirked that evil smiled and said, "Don't worry, we're not here to start a fight." Then that evil smirk turned into a grin. "Or are we, hoodlum?" He said, taking a sip of his whisky bottle.

John's fist started to clutch, and he started to clench his jaw. Alex's eyes started to fill with fear; they got wider, and he got whiter than a sheep.

Then we heard someone yell "John!" from the right side of us. We turned, and it was Dan and Jess speedwalking toward us.

Chris faced them and started to say "Well, isn't it little miss—" till Jessie got close to him and popped him in the nose, and he fell backward on his butt. We all looked at her, and she looked at us.

"Are you guys okay?" she asked, rubbing the fist that she threw at Chris.

John scanned her a few times then said, "Um, are you okay?" He was bug-eyed and confused.

She smiled. "Yeah, don't worry," she said, putting her hands behind her so we couldn't see the one she used.

But Dan saw it and said, carefully grabbing her hand, "No, you're not." It was a little red, but it wasn't bleeding or anything. But Dan didn't care. It was really red to him. He carefully rubbed it, and Jessie just let him.

Then Chris got back up and said, "You little—"

Dan pushed him back down before he could finish. Chris's friends started to walk up to him, trying to act all tough. But compared to Dan, they weren't even tough or tougher. So they should probably back down.

Then Dan said, "You get any closer I'm gonna drop you like a bag."

Once they heard that, they didn't get any closer than they already were and helped Chris up. And he said, "You're right, hood, we should probably *wait till the rumble*!" He wiped the blood off his nose.

I started to think, *I don't ever want to make Jessie mad.* Dan's mind went to sea for a few seconds.

"Wait..." He paused to look at us. "There's going to be a rumble?" Then he looked back at Chris, who was glaring at him. "Since when and what day?" He was now looking back and forth at us.

Chris didn't say anything, and neither did his friends. They just jumped into the flaming Mustang and drove off in a flash. John sighed and told him when, where, and that we needed as many guys as possible. Dan put on a big smile. He liked rumbles, mostly because he liked to throw a bunch of kids around and make them scared of him.

"Sounds good to me, Johnny, I'll be there."

I saw Jessie's blue eyes get wide. "What? No," she said, worriedly. We looked at her like she was cursing at us. Dan gave her a weird and confused look. She whined at us. "I don't want you to get hurt," she moaned.

Dan's weird and confused look faded away, and his lip dropped a little. "Hey, I won't get hurt." He walked over and put his hand on the back of her neck. She looked at Dan with those beautiful big blue eyes. Dan seemed to freeze up inside and get lost.

Then John ruined it. "Yeah, he throws those kids around like nothing," he said as he chuckled.

Jessie smiled at him. "John?"

"Yeah?"

"Shut up and stop acting like Mark."

John smiled like a child at her. Then she and Dan got back to talking. But they were talking really quiet, where I could barely hear them.

After they sat there for a little while, they walked us to Alex's parents' house. As we walked, Jessie had her left arm around Dan's torso, and Dan had his right arm around Jessie's shoulders. They were whispering and giggling as they did a little sway and nudged each other. I knew they had only known each other for a little over a week, but they already seemed in love with each other. And a little over a week ago, Dan was playing football at the park with us and lying underneath a blue-eyed girl with long blond curly hair, and we got all hyper when we realized he liked her. Isn't it funny how a man and a woman can fall in love with each other without having to satisfy one another or try to be what they're not to make the other fall in love with them and be happy with what they're not? Another thing that is funny is how long they can love each other. I mean, how can people last their whole life with someone without getting tired of them or getting bored with the same person? I guess that's what love is, and what Dan and Jessie are. A man and a woman so in love with each other even if they've only known each other for a little over a week. Probably because they're honest with each other, but that might change.

Not trying to say that one of them lies to the other and they break up with each other. I mean, maybe if they cheat on the other, then yeah, they should break up or try to work it out. But I doubt that they would cheat on each other. What I'm trying to say is that, like I said before, Dan loves, and I mean loves, rumbles. So I don't know if he will keep Jessie's promise that he made to her before we left.

Once we got to Alex's parents' house, his mom was happy to see Dan and Jessie with us. She was so excited that she gave them a hug, and they hugged her back. Alex's mom was a nice small woman with black wavy hair and green eyes and a sweet smile. Alex looks just like her. Except he has his dad's dark-brown eyes. His dad and mine have known each other for a long time, even before Dan was born. Just like our moms, they'd known each other since preschool. They were all like sisters. So when our mom died, they were devastated. We all were devastated that she left our lives. We're all pretty much family when it comes to how long we've known each other. Even some of our grandparents knew each other.

We left after fifteen minutes passed by, but this time I was in front of Dan and Jessie. They started to whisper and giggle to each other. I wanted to turn around and see what they were doing, but I didn't want them to give me a weird look. So I just listened to them. Although I didn't know what they were saying to each other, I could tell they were flirting and kissing each other's cheeks, or at least Dan was. 'Cause Jessie kept telling him to stop. But he didn't, till we got to the house, and they stopped giggling. But they kept holding each other. When we walked in, Matt, Bradley, David, and George were sitting on the couch. When they saw us, I could tell that something was wrong. They were all surrounding Matt, who was bawling his eyes out.

Once Jessie saw him, she ran and sat on the couch next to him. "What's wrong Matt?" She turned him toward her. Matt looked away from her, but she grabbed his chin and turned his face to her. Matt sniffled and wiped some of his tears from his cheeks.

"My, my girl…girlfriend…ch-cheated on…me." He was trying so hard not to cry.

Jessie's eyes got wide with anger. "What? She cheated on you?" Matt nodded his head up and down slowly. "Oh, that little dirty…" And she started to call Matt's ex-girlfriend every dirty word that you could call a bad teenage girl. After she was done, we all looked at her amazed. Oh, except Bradley. Bradley was laughing his heart out. She looked at him. "Bradley, shut up, and you guys stop looking at us." Bradley stopped laughing or at least tried. But Jessie didn't care and got back to Matt. "Matt…" she said. Matt looked at her with trembling lips. "Listen to me," she said, putting both her hands on his cheeks. "Forget about that girl. If you keep thinking about her, you won't get over her." Then she put her hands in her lap. Matt looked away from her.

"But she—"

And out of nowhere Jessie yelled, "For crying out loud, Matt, she cheated on you! She doesn't love or like!" She slammed her hands on her legs then sighed when Matt said, "Just like every girl," looking at her with a nonjoyful look in his eyes. "I'm sorry, kiddo, but you really need to realize that you're still young."

Matt glared at her. "That's what every girl thinks. I'm young, I'm a child, I need to grow up. I swear no girl likes me in this town." It got quiet in the house. No one said anything.

Till Dad walked in through the door, happy as could be. Then he saw all of us surrounding Matt, who was trying so hard not to cry. He dropped his work bag and walked over to us. "Hey, what's going on, little man?" he asked as he stood in front of Matt.

Matt looked down at his feet then said, "Kathy cheated on me." He was sobbing with every word.

Kathy had been with Matt for a long while. At least five or six weeks. Kathy wasn't the nicest girl in the world, but Matt loved her, and we weren't about to tell him that we didn't like her or that she was bad news. So we waited till he knew, and now I wish we had told him she wasn't the right girl. 'Cause now he's bawling his eyes out for her, and when Matt cries that bad about a girl, he really loves her, but they seem to break his heart like glass and shatter it on the ground, making it seem like it was nothing to them.

Once Dad heard the word *cheated*, his face went from concerned to fierce. "She cheated on you?"

Matt nodded his head. "Uh hum."

Dad stood there, mouth upon, still fierce. Then he sat down on the other side of Matt. "I'm sorry, little man," he said as he putted Matt on the back and rubbed. "There's other girls out there."

Matt wiped off the trails of tears on his cheeks and said, "Yeah, but none like her." He was starting to ease down.

Dad smiled. "Well, there might be a few girls out there that are cheaters and act like they love you, like her." He stopped rubbing his back and put his hands on his knees. "But they'll all lead you to the right girl. Like how they led me to your mother, Now she was sure a stubborn young lady at the time." He lifted one eyebrow and pointed at Matt. "Oh, and like how they led Dan to Jessie."

Dan gave Dad a weird look. "What do ya mean I haven't dated in three or four years?"

Dad smiled at him like he didn't know what Dan was saying and said, "Yeah, because you work too long and too hard to have one."

"Exactly." Dan smiled.

"Yeah, exactly, you were lonely and stubborn." Now he looked at Dan then added, "Stubborn like your mother."

"I was not stubborn."

"Yes, you were, like your mom."

"No, I wasn't, Dad."

"Uh hum," Dad said, still cocking one eyebrow at Dan.

Dan rolled his eyes at Dad and said, "All right, whatever you say, old man." He was grinning happily. Dad now raised both of his eyebrows.

"What did you say, little man?" Dad was getting up off the couch. Dan was starting to get tough with Dad. This meant they were going to get rough with each other, and when they do, Dad usually wins. Dan says he lets him win because Dad's getting old and fragile. When Dad heard him say that, he laughed and told him that he was the one that was getting old and fragile. Dad and Dan have always been playfully rough with each other since Dan was thirteen years old and able to fight or wrestle around with him. They've always been close to each other. Makes sense since they were exactly alike in every way, from their looks to their dark, tuff dirty blonde hair. A lot of people thought they were brothers by how young Dad looks, or looked, because now he has light and dark gray hairs coming through that are starting to show his age. But Dad still has a good-looking bod for an old guy.

"You heard me, old man," he said slowly, in a playful way. Dad started to chuckle.

"Say that one more time, little man," he said, putting up one finger.

Jessie looked at Dan, as if saying "Don't do it, you're going to get your butt kicked." But he didn't listen and started to say "Old—" but he only got that far till Dad grabbed him and knocked him on the ground and put him in a headlock.

"Are ya gonna say it again, huh, are ya?"

"Old man!" Dan said, laughing as his face got bright red.

Then Dad let go of him and said, "You little turd." He slapped Dan in the back of the head. Dan turned to him as Dad got up.

"Yep, old man, I am a turd," he said with a big grin.

Dad couldn't help but laugh at him and say, "Stop calling me that, boy." He put his hands on his knees as he bent over.

Dan gave him one more silly grin and said, "Okay, old man, I will." Everyone started to grin at him. Even Matt was grinning happily. Jessie gave Dan a look that said, "Stop making fun of your dad." I guess Dan knew what that look meant and said, "All right, little woman."

But he shouldn't have said that 'cause Jessie now gave him a death stare and said, "Don't call me 'little woman,' Danny."

Dan sat there, smiling like a child. "Okay…" But then he hesitated for a few seconds then said, "Never mind, I don't want to end up like your brother Jason." Jessie smiled at him, and we looked at him with curiosity in our eyes. "You wanna know why?" He looked at all of us. "Well, one day he said something a little dirty, and she hit him in the head with a small pan," Dan said with a funny look. We all were laughing. I never knew Jessie would be so mean to anybody. Besides the high-class kids who got away with everything that we didn't.

Matt seemed to feel a lot better after a while, with everyone making jokes and talking about the good old days and all the weird things we'd been through. Bradley had been through a lot of weird things, by his crazy, odd girl stories he was telling us. Dad was telling us about the good ole days. The days when we were all younger. The days when Mom was alive, when me and Dad didn't fight. Although, he and I hadn't been fighting for a while since that talk we had in his old beat-up red work truck. The only time he actually yelled at me was when we got in that big sock fight with those high-class kids who scattered like frightened rats when Robert and his cop buddies came to the scene, while he took us and Blake Frederick to the police station. There officially wasn't enough room to fit us and Blake's whole gang in the two police cars. So they just grabbed Blake, who was the leader of his gang, to answer their questions.

Blake had about twenty guys in his group of hoodlums. Out of every gang in town, his was the meanest, the toughest, and the strongest. But out of his gang, he was the meanest, the toughest, and the strongest hoodlum. When he was around girls, he would say the most inappropriate things to them. That when they turned around, their jaw would be down on the ground, and their eyes would be as big as ping-pong balls. Blake would grin and start laughing. Then once they turned around, he would start talking inappropriate again and do things that I don't and can't say. To me, Blake was not good news. But I remember what Mom told me when I was younger. "Don't always judge people by their actions or how they treat other people. Because someone hurt them really bad or someone took something away from them and made them dark and cold inside and sometimes in the outside." I knew why she told me that. It was because I asked her why some people were so mean to others, and that was what she told me. So I never judged someone at all even if I hated their guts. I never tried to make them sour or tried to tick them off 'cause I didn't know what they had been through.

CHAPTER 11

The rumble was today. The day of blood and teeth flying everywhere. The day of fighting and knockouts to end a feud. Although it isn't going to fix much if we win or not. It's just going to be fine for a few weeks. Till the rich kids get bored and get into one of their Mustang and find one of us kids to mug.

The day of this rumble is where Dan can't go only because he made a promise to Jessie. I think it's a good thing that he isn't going. Only because he needs to stop going to the rumbles and so he doesn't lose Jessie. I mean, if he keeps going to rumbles, Jessie will probably get tired of it and get up and leave. But I doubt that will happen. She's too in love with him to leave him. To be honest with you, I'm surprised that he isn't going to the rumble. Like I said before, Dan loves a rumble. It's pretty much the only time he can knock people off their feet and let off steam.

Matt is still a little teary-eyed from yesterday. When his girlfriend, Kathy, cheated on him. He's better now but doesn't smile as much. Jessie started to joke around with him yesterday, saying, "Do you want me to go and beat this chick up? I will, you just tell me where she lives and I'll beat the brat outta her."

Matt smiled at the ground but didn't say anything for a while, then said, "It's fine, I'll just forget about her."

Jessie mussed his hair up and said, "Okay, kid, but if she is bugging you, you just go and tell me, all right."

"All right, Jess, I will," Matt said with a light smile.

Jessie can make anyone smile if she really wants to or if they're having a bad day. Now that I think about it, Jessie's pretty much like our mom. She's always giving us some advice or cheering us up and picks us up from school and telling the high-class kids off. One time she saw them and gave them the finger. Which Matt, Mark, and Bradley thought was pretty funny. On my birthday, she bought me the shoes I wanted, which were Converse, black-and-white Converse that were $10. Not only that, she took me and Matt shopping one time and told us, "I'm going to show you how it is done, boys." After, we had a deep conversation about how we need more clothes and stuff. She also helps us with are homework too. At least when we need it.

But it seems that she has a little bit of spunk to her now that we know her a lot better. She probably didn't want to put off a bad impression on us or anyone else. To be honest, she is a little bit different from girls in our town. She seems to have a bit of a country hick in her. Well, she is from Texas, so I guess that explains it. But that isn't all we learned about her. We learned that she was a rodeo queen and went to veterinary school for two years, but then she decided that wasn't her thing, to help animals. So she moved here to become a preschool teacher. Which suits her 'cause she's good with kids. Well, at least teenagers in fact.

She and Dan seem to be really attached now and act really, really weird around each other. Dad told us that they're at that stage where they really, really, really just can't wait to be alone with each other.

Talking about Dad, he seems to be really happy lately. Might be because Jessie and Dan are together and happy. He barely yells at me ever since he met Jess. He's also happy that I've been talking about doing track or football next year too, which seems fun to do now that I'm fifteen. It didn't seem fun when I was fourteen.

Another thing that I noticed is that I'm getting interested in girls now. I just can't help looking at their curves and how their dress show all their curves and how skinny their waist is. The one thing that makes me go crazy is when they wear shorts with tank tops that show their belly and when they give me that look.

Now let me tell you how I found out girls came to my mind and how I figured out I had started my puberty. One time we were walking, and a couple of girls passed by, and Bradley and Mark started to check them out, you know the usual. Till this one girl looked me straight in the eyes, and I started to get that feeling in my stomach again, and my heart started to race as I scanned her curves. I about stared at her for ten seconds till John slapped me hard in the back of the head as he said, "Stop checking girls out." I didn't say anything to him. Only because I realized that I was checking out girls, and I was afraid of getting embarrassed. But then John said "Wait" and stopped us. "You were checking out girls." He smirked at me. Oh boy, I thought. I knew what was coming, or at least I thought I knew what was coming. "Did you start puberty?" he said, still smiling at me. My heart stopped racing at the word *puberty*, so I sat there thinking about what I should say. Till I finally muttered, "Um, I…I don't know." I was trying to hide in my jacket. Still John smiled at me, which kind of freaked me out a little bit, and said "I think you did, 'cause you're not acting yourself, boy." We started to walk again.

That night I thought really hard about what John said. I knew that he was right that I probably did start puberty, not only because I started to like girls and wanted to do football and track, but I was also getting facial hair and hair in other places too. But that's not it. I also grew about three inches, and my voice was starting to change also. At least that was what everybody told me. It happened when I walked out of my room and into the living room, where Dad and Matt were sitting on the couch, and I said "Good morning" as I took a stepped out of the hallway. When I said that, Dad looked up from his newspaper, and Matt looked away from the television, with their jaws dropped. Then Mark, Clark, and Bradley stepped out of the kitchen with their jaw dropped, but Bradley was blinking frantically. It was quiet, and everyone was staring at me, making me feel all awkward standing there looking at them, not knowing what in the world was going on, so I asked one word, "What?"

They stood there for a few seconds, then Clark said, "Your voice…"

Then Mark finished his sentence. "It changed."

I looked at them surprised and said, "Really."

"Yeah, like, it's really deep," Bradley said.

"How deep?" I asked.

"Like Dan deep," Matt said.

I smiled and started for the kitchen. Once I got to Mark, he stopped me and put me in front of him. Then that was when I noticed I was the same height as him.

"Holy moly, kid, you're the same height as me," he said, looking me up and down. "And just to think, you were to my nose just a few weeks ago." He let go of me. "You're scaring me, boy, you really are scaring me. I mean, come here, Matt and Mr. D."

Matt came running over, but Dad just said, "Don't rub it in, Mark." He looked back at his newspaper. Something was wrong with him. He wasn't excited like them. He was more depressed than excited.

But once Matt got to me, his eyes got wide, and he yelled, "You're taller than me, little brother!" We all burst out laughing. "What are you peek tons laughing at? My little brother is taller than me. Look at us all."

Bradley came up to him and, putting his arm around Matt, and said, "Yeah, like a half an inch, my friend." Matt looked at him still surprised.

"Yeah, but he was like to the bottom of my eyes about two week ago," he said, walking toward me. Bradley smiled and shook his head at him.

"Whatever."

Matt gave him a tick of look and said, "Oh, you just wait till your little brother is taller than you." But Bradley just kept smiling at him.

"Yeah right, my little brother isn't going to be taller than me," he said as he grabbed George, who just got out of the bathroom "I mean, look at him, he's as short as a dwarf." He rubbed his little brother's hair. That day everyone seem to be surprised about how much taller and how deep my voice was. Not only that, but it really made me think about my dad.

Was it because he was mad about something, or was it because he knew I was growing up? I don't know, but something was on his mind that day.

But anyways, Blake's gang and our gang were going to the rumble to stump those rich kids tonight and together as one. The only ones that weren't going were Dan and Alex because Alex's mom didn't want anything more to happen to him, and Jessie didn't want Dan to get hurt or worse, but we all knew that no one could hurt Super Dan because he was strong like a bull. But I didn't know if this Super Dan bull would stay put like his little woman told him to, 'cause she loves him and cares about him and doesn't want him to get hurt or worse. But like I said before, this bull couldn't get easily hurt because he was Super Dan. But I think he should stay with Jessie. So then maybe they can go on a date or something romantic together.

Right now I just hope he does stay put, 'cause he and Jessie have something that's more than just a spark. We all were going to meet up on the far west side of the park at about 8:30 or 9:00 p.m. Which was the time where a lot of people went to bed. So it made it perfect to have a rumble.

But before I went to the rumble, I was going to go see Alex and then Jessie. After that, I would go and get some flowers. Then go to the graveyard to go see Mom's grave for a while then go home and get ready for the rumble. I like where Mom is buried. She's under a medium-size oak tree out of the rain, the most perfect and peaceful place to read a book.

As I walked to Alex's house, I felt big drops of rain fall on the back of my neck and slide to the front and drip off, or it would stay there, and I would have to wipe it off, and then another drop of rain would get stuck or would drip off. For some reason, I kind of liked the rain dripping onto my neck then on to the ground. It felt good how, when it hits my skin, it instantly cools on my neck, and how when it slides down my neck, it absorbs all the heat from it. Then it falls to the ground or clings on to it, making it where I have to wipe it off.

Once I got there, his mom immediately let me in, more like yanked me inside from the rain. I heard her whisper underneath her breath, "What in the world are you doing out here in this weather, Mike?"

I shrugged, not knowing what to tell her. But I was used to rainy weather here. It didn't bug me.

Me and Alex went to his room and started to talk about the rumble and Dan an him not being able to go to it. Alex told me that he was happy that his mom didn't let him go because his rib cage started to hurt, and he didn't want to break his nose even more. He also told me that I looked older than usual and reminded him of Dan and Dad a little bit by how tall I was getting and how deep my voice had gotten. I stayed at Alex's house for about an hour. Then went to Jessie's house and got a snack there. Dan wasn't there because he was working, but Jessie was there. We talked for a little bit and stuff, till Dan came through the door about thirty minutes into mine and Jessie's conversation. And we all started to talk to each other.

After that I said goodbye to them and walked to the flower shop and got Mom's favorite flowers, which were orchids, and went on my way to the graveyard. Once I got there, I went to the medium-size oak tree where Mom was and sat the flowers on the grave. I started to talk to her as if she were standing right there in front of me. Man, I really miss mom. She was a good woman, too good of a woman to die, but she did, and that's the shocker. I started to read the words on the stone and looked at the picture of her that was in the stone with a piece of glass over it to keep it getting wet from the rain. I forgot how beautiful Mom looked before she passed away. She was as beautiful as those orchids that I sat on her grave.

I sat there crouching by her grave, talking to her about Jessie and how she and Dan were so in love, even though it had only been a month. Then some people walked by me and gave me weird looks. I started to think they might've thought I was crazy because I was talking to a grave. But they didn't know who was in this grave and how important she was to me. My mom meant the world to me, and now she isn't in this world anymore. She's in a better world now where no one judges anyone. Hopefully she is, but I know she is. She was the kindest, most beautiful, amazing woman in this world, and hopefully she is in that world too.

I sat up and noticed it wasn't raining so hard any more, but it was sprinkling, and I noticed from a far distance a rainbow forming behind the trees. I couldn't help but smile at it. Maybe today at the rumble we might win and avenge Alex for what those high-class kids did to him. And we were going to hit them hard tonight.

I finally started to walk back home with my head down and hiding between my shoulders and my hood in a mysterious way. Although I wasn't cold or anything.

The only parts of me that were cold were my ears, my nose, and my cheeks. It was still sprinkling when I got home at four thirty. And to burn up some time, I made myself a sandwich, watched *M*A*S*H** for about an hour and a half. Then went to my bedroom to sleep for a couple of hours. That was when I noticed that I was growing out of my bed and needed a new one. But I decided that I'd do that when we had the money and the time to get me a new bed.

I about slept for an hour and a half, till I heard noises coming from the kitchen and the living room and realized we had about thirty minutes till the rumble.

Which gave me enough time to wake a little bit. When I went out of my bed room and into the hall, I saw the whole gang in the living room and kitchen. George saw me and said, "Bradley told me you grew a little bit."

I smiled at him tiredly and said, "Yeah."

He grinned back at me and said, "Your voice has also gotten deeper and more manly too."

I looked at him like I already did know that and told him, "Tell me about it." I started for the kitchen, till Dad popped the door open with his big work bag over his shoulder. He looked at us and took a big sigh and said, "Now you boys be careful tonight, all right." He was putting his big work bag on the counter.

"No problem, Mr. D, no problem at all," said Mark, sounding buzzed up already from just seven beers. Like you heard before, Mark is the bad one, not as bad as Blake though. Mark is the little party animal out of us. He always keeps the chaos going on and makes the most inappropriate jokes you'll ever hear in your life. But the joke isn't the worst part of it; it's the way people react to it. Some burst out laughing, which are usually the people like Mark and Bradley. The ones that sit there and grin at him are usually the responsible ones that like to have a little fun.

And the ones that straight up slap him in the head are the too-good-for-you kind of girls. The girls that all the guys in our town could have as a girlfriend but know they are too good for them because they are the sweet, innocent, nonparty girls who don't even know they are beautiful. And we're the mean, non-innocent, crazy guys who will not be anything more than a hood. At least that's what rich adults say about us. But they don't know our future, and besides, the rich kids are pretty much as bad as us. They're just richer than us and have more opportunities in life and more chances too. Only because they're from a rich family, a rich town, and know a lot of rich people too. All their lives are about money and being rich and better than everyone else, sometimes even friends. Which was the most strange thing of being a rich kid.

I mean, why would you like your friends then hate your friends all because you thought you were better than them? But no one is better than anyone or anything, even if you're rich. 'Cause if you're rich, you're a snotty little brat who gets whatever you want, and if you're a low-class kid, you always get in trouble for everything, even things that you didn't do, which is how you start to get mean and do those things that they accuse you of doing.

So I guess there isn't such a thing as better people, but there is such a thing as good people. Sometimes it is hard to notice and hard to find that they're nice and good people. But if you really go deep down in their cold heart, you might be able to find a bit of kindness, and maybe you can help that kindness grow and show them that not everybody takes them for their looks or where they're from or who they're family is and stuff like that. Maybe you could change their mind about life and show them that there is a bit of sunshine in this cold, rocky earth of ours and that life isn't something you try your best at then throw it away or give up on, but that you can do so much more with it than be told you're something that you're not, and if you are, that you can change it and prove everyone wrong and prove you're more than that. You just have to try really hard to accomplish it.

After we watched a couple of shows for about twenty-five minutes, it was time, and we were all pumped up and ready to kick some butt tonight, and together as one, we will stump those stupid high-class kids.

I was a little sad that Alex and Dan couldn't come, but Alex is hurt, and Jessie doesn't want Dan to get hurt. Like that would ever happen. No one, and I mean no one can beat Dan.

A lot of guys have tried, but they either ended up losing most of their teeth or having a concussion or having broken bones. Oh, that reminds me of one thing that Dan did that was bad. Although he started at seventeen and stopped at eighteen, and now he didn't give up; he stopped because Mom and Dad found out that he was going to one-on-one rumbles and told him it was time for him to grow up, even though he was already grown-up enough. But he needed to stop only because he started to go down the wrong road. But as you can see, he found the right road again and hopefully he stays on that road.

Once we got to the west side of the park, where we would end this stupid high-class, low-class thing for now, we stopped and stood in front of Blake, and he said, "Hey, Matthew, Michael, and your friends." He looked at each one of us one at a time. "You boys ready?" We all nodded, and he gave us one of his evil-like smiles, then started to walk to his group of naughty delinquents from the wild, wild side of New York or the bad side of this town.

As we walked toward the group, I started to think about Dad then started to worry about him. He didn't tell us good luck or anything. Usually he does, even before Mom died. He would always say something before we went to a rumble. Was it something I did? Was it at my birthday party? Did he have cancer too and didn't want to tell us? I thought to myself. It might be something from the party. I noticed that Dad was a little blue during that time. Maybe he was just sick that day. I don't know. I started to think it was because I was about the same height as him, just a few more inches. Or maybe it was because my voice was deeper than usual. I really, really didn't know. All I knew was that I was worried about him. I didn't want to lose him too. He was my only parent left. I can't bear losing him too. I wouldn't survive without my dad.

Once I said that to myself, I thought how babyish and foolish I was being, but hey, I'm just worried about my dad. I mean Dad barely looks at me anymore, and I can't stand him not smiling. He's always blue now. I just don't know what's going on with him, and that's what worries me the most.

We found our spots in the small crowd of muscle men. I was in the back of everyone with George because Matt and Bradley didn't want us to get the first hit out of everybody. At least that was what they said, but it was pretty obvious that they didn't want us to get hurt. 'Cause in the front, everyone runs after the person in front of them and hits them as hard as they can. Some of us have learned to slide and dodge their hits.

George and I didn't want to sit all the way in the back. So we decided to move up a little. We started to walk closer to the front, when I saw a big guy, like Dan's size. I started to think it might be Dan, but it couldn't be Dan. He wouldn't break Jessie's promise, would he? I started to push through people, trying to see if it was Dan, and the closer I got, the more it looked like Dan.

No, it couldn't be Dan. He wouldn't ever lie to Jessie, would he? That question rushed through my mind like a rocket. Would he, would he? He can't. He loves Jessie. But I guess I forgot how much Dan loves rumbles. 'Cause once I got to the big-size-looking Dan, I slapped my hand on his shoulder and turned him around. It was Dan. Why in the world is he here? I guess that's also why Matt didn't want us to go up front too, I thought. 'Cause he tried to get me to back off, but I yanked away from him.

I was mad at Dan. He shouldn't be here; he should be with Jessie, snuggled on the couch with her, watching television. But no, he'd rather come here and fight with us. I know it doesn't seem like a big deal. You're probably, like, the more the merrier. But he's twenty-one now. He needs to grow up! Just like how Matt needs to know there's someone out there and doesn't need to cry about one chick. And like how I need to figure out what's going on with Dad. But hey, I guess we all have our own problems at one time.

I gave him a furious look and started to let it all out. "Why are you here, Dan?" I paused for a second. Then started back up again. "You should be at Jessie's house. You should go to Jessie's house!"

But Dan sat there quietly for a while then said, "Well, it's too late now, little brother." I knew I couldn't say anything back to him. Only because the high-class kids were already here and ready to take us on. "But don't worry about it, I'll talk to her, she'll understand." Till one of the high-class kids tried to punch me, but then cool, smooth Dan caught it before he could hit me, and he knocked him so hard that once he was on the ground, he didn't get back up. Everyone was so surprised that their mouths literally dropped to the ground, and the rich kids took a few steps back.

Then everyone, rich kids and not-so-rich kids, ran after each other and rammed one another. As they ran and rammed each other, I heard George yell "*Here we go!*" As he ran and jumped on someone. When I socked a rich kid, the kid that Dan knocked out got up. Well, at least for a moment. because he was too dizzy and fell back down on the ground. But then he sat up for a while till his eyes stopped spinning and got back on his feet. Now that really cracked me up and made my day even better. Till someone punched me in the middle of my back, and a shot of pain went up and down my spine, but I didn't fall to my knees. Instead I turned around and elbowed him in the face, making him fall down on the ground and made him get a bloody nose. At that, I was surprised how much I could hurt someone. But I kind of enjoyed it. Now I know why Dan loves it so much.

CHAPTER 12

After the rumble was over, we started to walk to Jessie's house. When we got there, Jessie was standing right in front of the door, folding her arms, and boy, let me tell you, she didn't look too happy. I noticed that Jessie's brothers' wives were sitting behind her on the couch, and they didn't look too happy nether. We all knew why Jessie wasn't happy. We gave Dan a look that meant, "You're in big, big trouble, man." But Dan already knew he was in big, big trouble by the look on his face. He knew he was going to get his butt kicked for breaking the promise that he made to Jessie.

After sitting there for at least five seconds, Jessie finally said, trying to keep calm, "I thought you said you weren't going to go." But Dan didn't say anything. He just sat there looking dumb, all big bug-eyed with his face getting red. Jessie glared at him and said, "Well, aren't you gonna say anything?" She put her hands on her hips. Dan sat there with his mouth open, but no words came out. So Jessie's brothers walked over and tried to tell her why he did it. But she snapped at them. "No, you guys stay out of it!" And they backed off.

Finally Dan managed to say, "I'm sorry I broke your promise, but I wasn't just going to let my little brothers go out there and fight without me. They never fought in a rumble without me." He walked closer to her. "Now I know that sounds like a lame excuse, but it's the truth, okay." He paused for a few seconds then continued. "Now, I promise that I won't go to another rumble again, okay." He put his hands on her shoulders. I knew what Dan was trying to do. He was trying to flatter her and sweet talk her. But he would keep his promise or at least try to.

Jessie stopped glaring at him and said, "You promise?" sounding calmer.

Dan started to smile and said, "I promise." Then he rubbed her naked shoulders with his thumbs. She smiled and wrapped her arms around him. When Dan hugged her back, he said, "Unless I have to," as he started to grin happily.

Then she pinched him on the back. But he just laughed and took a step back from her. He pulled her closer to give her a kiss. But she kept pushing away from him and telling him to stop. I noticed that they didn't fight for very long, like I thought, and that's a good thing too. 'Cause I guess that means they understand and trust each other.

"Okay," Dan started to say, "if you're not going to kiss me on the lips, then give me a smooch on the cheek, then I'll stop." He pointed at his cheek.

She pulled her eyebrows up and said, putting up one finger, "Just one smooch on the cheek."

"Uh-huh," he replied as he nodded then turned his cheek toward her. Just when I thought he wasn't going to turn his face back, guess what happens. He turned his face back and kissed her right on the lips, and Jessie slapped him on the arm before he could run off. George and I started to look at each other. We both knew what we were thinking. That is, Dan and Jess were getting a little too flirtatious, if you know what I mean.

We looked at Matt and all of them, but they just smiled at us, which confused both of us by the look on their faces. Bradley put his hands on each of our shoulders and said, "Um, I think we should probably leave you two alone." He started to pull us back to the door.

Then Justin said, "Yeah, honey, let's go home so we can leave these two lovebirds alone." He grabbed his wife's hand and started to walk out the door.

"Right behind you," Joseph said as his wife walked toward him, smiling.

After Jessie's brothers and their wives walked out, we started out the door. George and I were the last ones out. So we both saw Dan and Jessie look at each other then run upstairs to Jessie's bedroom. I couldn't stop thinking of what they might do up there.

After Jessie's brothers left with their wives and kids, we heard a squeal. So, George and I looked up to see what was going on. When we did, Dan was taking off his shirt and jumping on the bed with Jessie. Before we could see them start to kiss, John grabbed our T-shirts and said, "Get your guys' butts up in front of us and stop staring at them." He pushed us to the front of everybody. But me and him just had to take one last look. I wish I didn't look.

The whole way home me and George didn't say anything. We even didn't say anything when we got there too. I guess Dad noticed that we weren't saying anything by the looks he gave us. Usually he and I talk a lot at dinner. Dad started to glare at us.

"What in the world is wrong with you boys?" he said in a surprisingly calm voice. We all started to look at each other, trying to see who was going to be brave enough to tell him. Then Dad yelled, "What's going on with you boys?" He sat up "Did something bad happen at the rumble?" He was glaring even more.

Matt took a deep breath and said, "No, Dad, it's just that… um…well…" Then he looked at George and me. Then back at Dad. "How in the world can I say this without those two getting a weird vibe?" He put one hand on his forehead and thumbed us with the other.

Dad started to grind his teeth as he looked at George and me. "Is he laying her down tonight, boys?"

Our eyes got big, and I got chills. Then Matt yelled "Dad!" lifting his head back up.

Mark burst out laughing, Dad started to chuckle, John sat on the couch acting like he wasn't hearing any of this, and poor little George sat there with a frozen look on his face as he tried to watch television, with his eyes wider than ever, twitching his nose, with food still in his mouth.

After that, everybody went home without a word. But John said goodbye to us. I sat on my bed with the words "laying her down" still sitting in my mind. But then I started to think, what was it like to have a girlfriend? What was it like to have someone as gorgeous as Jessie laying on your chest when you wake up? I might not ever know, or at least I won't know for a while till a girl would ask me how old I am and take me somewhere where we'll be alone. At least that's what I think might happen when I lose my boyhood to some girl who doesn't have a lot of money but has a lot of love to give to any virgin boy who wants to know what love is, like me.

CHAPTER 13

The next day I woke up still a little weirded out and terrified a bit from last night.

It's just odd to think what they did that night. It's just not right that that's how you make babies. Then a crazy thought broke through my mind. What if he got her pregnant? Oh man, I'm not ready to be an uncle, I thought to myself. Nah, Dan probably didn't. Hopefully he didn't.

Another thing that was killing me that morning was that the house was quieter than ever, again. The only noise was the sizzling of the bacon on the pan that was on the burning stovetop. One thing that was creeping the jeepers out of me was the creepy look Mark was giving me as I was trying to finish my homework. I wanted him to stop but didn't know how to tell him. That was how creeped out I was.

Then after about four or five minutes passed, I finally got so creeped out that I yelled, "Will you please stop looking at me like that?" I dropped my pencil and put my hands on the table. But of course he asked "Why?" I slapped my forehead and said, "Because you're scaring the crude out of me."

He smiled at me and asked, "I made you poop your pants?" He cracked up.

I slapped my forehead again for the last time as if to say "You're retarded, Mark, you really are." Then actually said, "You've been drinking, haven't you."

He smiled at me and said, "Yep, I have, for sure."

Things started to get a little better, till the door opened and Dan appeared behind it and said, "Oh, hello."

Oh no, I thought as he walked over to me and sat down in the chair by me. *Play it cool, Mike, just play it cool and don't talk about last night neither,* I told myself. But guess what I say after telling myself to not talk about last night. I go on and say, "So how was your night, Dan?" *So much for trying to keep it cool. Now everyone is looking at you, Mike.*

An awkwardness filled the kitchen and the living room. I tried to hide in between my shoulders like a frightened turtle but couldn't because I don't have the same bone structure as a turtle.

Dan smiled at me and said, "I was just about to talk about last night."

I looked at him, saying, "Oh please don't tell me how your night went with Jessie. Please don't be like Matt and tell me how you did it with her. I'm only fifteen years old, Dan, please don't tell me how it went. I'm your little brother."

Of course Matt rushed over to hear what happened that night. Dan looked at him, saying, "Are you stupid, Matt?" Matt sat there patiently waiting to hear what Dan had to say about last night. Dan sighed and rolled his eyes and said, "We didn't do anything last night, Matt." He started to smile again as Matt's smile faded away.

"You know I got in trouble last night, remember, the rumble that I promised Jessie that I wasn't going to go to."

A sign of relief blew right through me as a rush of fear ran out of me. I was glad that nothing happened last night, only because that meant she can't get pregnant.

Although she has been a little grumpy lately, but maybe she just started her womanly problem or something. If you know what I'm talking about, good, but if you don't, don't expect me to tell you what it is or explain it to you. It's too disgusting to explain it or even tell you what it is. All I can say is that I'm glad I'm a boy. It would suck to be a girl. You get womanly problems that make you moody or emotional, and you have to push out a baby too, which I'm not so fond about.

Then I began to wonder, does it hurt to have a baby? I mean, some babies come out pretty big. Whatever, I'm just glad I don't have to go through all that and that I'm a boy, not a girl. But without girls, men wouldn't have someone to make their life complete or have someone make them smile or a pretty face to wake up to or someone to teach them how to dance.

Dan looked at all of us, like he was making sure we were all listening to what he had to say. "Besides, little brother, we already did it." The room got loud with laughter, and I got filled with embarrassment as my gut twisted and my head started to ache. "Do you wanna know how I did it?" I started to gag when he asked that. "Well, I played the song 'When a Man Loves a Woman' by Percy Sledge." He paused to bite his lip. "Man, that song really turns her on. You know that?"

Gosh, why did he say that. Now everyone is laughing at me, I said to myself as they laughed at me, loudly and proudly. Now I like making people laugh, but not if they're laughing at something I did. It just embarrasses me, and I don't like to be embarrassed. The only one that wasn't was Dad. Something is still wrong with him, but what, what makes him so blue? It still worried me.

Dan put a hand on my shoulder and said, "I'm sorry, little brother, didn't mean to make you gag yourself."

I looked at him and threw his hand off my shoulder and said, "Get your hand off me, you sicko." Everyone started laughing at me all over again. Till Dad let out a thundering yell, "Shut your mouths and leave him alone, boys!" And they did. They always listen to my dad because they know he will kick their butts if they don't. Besides, our dad is pretty much their dad, and they respect that.

Then Dad turned back around to take the baking off the pan. Something was up with Dad. First he acted all blue; second, he didn't even look or talk to me anymore; third, he started to stay up at night. That really worried me to see him like this. He must be hiding something from me, but why? And what was he hiding from me? I wish I knew, 'cause it hurt to see Dad like this. Only because I was so mean to him after Mom died, it makes me feel terrible for all the negative things I said about him and thought about him. I don't want anything to happen to my dad, my only parent left and that I have. I would cry for him like some kind of puppy if anything happened to him.

After breakfast, Dad had to leave for work. "One of you boys do the dirty dishes, and someone help dry them off, okay."

"Got it, Dad," Dan said, turning around to Dad, who was standing by the door.

"Okay, Mr. D, no problem," said Clark said.

I wanted to say something but didn't know what to say. So I sat there and stared at him with pleading eyes, waiting to see if he would look back at me, even if it was for just a second. He probably was going to look at me for one second, but at least he looked at me. I sat there for about ten seconds, till surprisingly, he glanced at me for a second, like I predicted. His eyes seemed to have a sad tone with a bit of pain in them. But then he quickly looked away and said goodbye as fast as possible and rushed out the door.

I felt a lump of pain stuck in my throat and asked myself a bunch of questions that ran all through my mind. What is wrong with him? Was it because of me? What did I do though? These questions I was asking myself made me angry, and the next thing I know is that I'm getting out of my chair and slamming it into the table and started walking off. Dan looked at me, ticked off. "Michael Jakob." But I didn't hear him over the pain of questions that made my mind spin like a twister.

I could hear Mark laughing in the background. But he started to stop, noticing how angry I was, and said, "M-Mike, you okay, buddy?" But I still didn't listen or say anything to them. I just hurried to my room and slammed the door behind me and locked it, and I grabbed the picture of me and Dad holding our fish up to the camera and crawled on my bed and lay down.

I heard the scooting of chairs and the rush of footsteps and them chattering to one another outside my door and them yelling my name. But their voices disappeared as I asked myself more and more questions. Did he find out that I did something bad? What was it that could have done that made him this way? Or maybe he lost his job? No, he couldn't have; he just went to work. Maybe something is bugging him? Then a terrifying question came to my mind. What if he is going to die?

No, I said to myself. It can't be. He can't die, not now. The thought of losing my dad, my only parent I have, scared me. I didn't want to lose my dad. I love my dad. I always have but never really had the chance to tell him. He was always there for me, there at football when I was I kid, there when Chris tried to jump me, and here now. Hopefully he will stay. I wouldn't stand him leaving me and my brothers. We had such a good time together till Mom passed away, and we were just getting better, and now he might die.

No, I'm not going to let that happen, not now when we got even with those high-class kids, and Jessie and Dan are more in love than Mom and Dad were. No, not now that I'm just getting started with my life and I'm just now starting to realize how much my dad means to me. Not now when I'm only fifteen. That's too early to lose your dad.

Tears filled my eyes like a fluid and drizzled down my cheeks. Then John said, "What's going on in there, you okay, little man?" I forgot they were out there and wiped off the tears and the wet trail they left behind.

"You're not mad, are you?" Bradley said, worriedly.

I looked from the picture and said, "No, I just want to be left alone for a while, that's all." It was quiet outside my door for a while.

Dan took a short sigh and said, "Oh, right, little brother." Then he started to talk to Matt. "When Dad gets back home, tell him he needs to talk to Mike, all right." Matt didn't say anything, so I guess he nodded. "I think Dad is making Mike worried about him."

"I will." Matt assured him that he would tell Dad. "Wait, why can't you?" he asked.

"Because me and Jessie are going on a date tonight at six o'clock, that's why."

"Can we come?" Mark asked with excitement.

"No, you guys went to the last two dates. Let us get some space, okay."

I started to smile when Mark and them started to whine at Dan, saying why they couldn't go with him and Jessie on their date, as they started to walk away from my bedroom door. I shook my head and looked back at the picture. Whatever happened to Dad and me? I questioned myself. Why don't we get along like we used to? I might not ever know.

I got out of my room only three times to get some food, go to the bathroom, and say goodbye to Dan before he left to go on his date with Jessie. After I went to the bathroom, I stayed in my room. I heard the door open and Dad come in and yawning. "Oh boy, what a day," he said.

Matt shuffled to his feet and say, "Hey, Dad, I need to talk to you about something."

There was a short silence before Dad said, "Sure, son, what's going on?"

Matt took in a deep breath and said "It's Mike…"

"What about him? What happened? Is he all right?" he said worriedly.

"Well, before you left, he seemed to be a little angry or something." Then another short silence went all through the house. Till Matt told Dad, "Dad, you really need to talk to him. He's worried about you, you know. He doesn't know what's going on. We all know but him, Dad."

"I know I need to, but I can barely talk to him without thinking he's Dan or someone else," he said as he sat on the couch. "Neither can I look at him without bawling my eyes out of the fact that my little boy is not a little boy anymore. And it frightens me how big he's gotten and how much of a man he's becoming, Matt."

That explains a lot of why he hasn't said anything to me or looked at me. He didn't like that I was looking like a true man and that I wasn't going to be his little boy anymore. Not to say I'm his youngest son and I think it would be hard to see your last kid becoming an adult. And I can't blame him for not saying anything to me 'cause he's a dad, and I'm not yet one and it's hard to see your baby getting ready to leave the nest.

But I was only glad that it wasn't something terrible, like Dad wasn't going to live any longer or Dad losing his job or worse.

I kept listening to their conversation, but the phone kept ringing about three or four times for Alex, George, Bradley, Mark, and Clark to go home. After ten minutes passed, John went home, and David said he was going to stay the night. Dad told him okay and gave him some blankets and pillows. Dad never really cares if any of the guys spend the night. As long as they clean up their mess, he's fine with it.

After that he turned off all the lights and opened my bedroom door and leaned on the threshold. I pretended I was asleep so he didn't have to tell me what was going on. Although I already knew what was going on with him. I wanted to wait for tomorrow to come for him to talk to me. Besides, I was tired tonight from being so lazy and listening to what everyone had to say. Before Dad left my room, I heard him whisper as he stood at the threshold, "Why do you have to grow up so fast, my boy?" He about stared at me for about thirty seconds before shutting my door and leaving like nothing happened.

But before he closed the door, I said, "I don't know, Dad." I didn't think he heard me, till he turned around as if a ghost just said something to him.

"What? Did you just say something, son?" He opened the door a little bit more to get a better look at me. I didn't say anything or open my eyes, but I smiled at him, letting him know it wasn't a ghost who said that but that it was his little boy. He tilted his head and smiled back at me. He shut my door, and David yelled "Good night, Mr. D" like a child. Dad chuckled and said, "Good night, David, see you in the morning, boy." He turned off the hallway light and walked to his bedroom. After that the house got quiet, and I closed my eyes and fell into a quiet, peaceful sleep.

CHAPTER 14

The next day everyone was still asleep when I woke up. I got dressed for the day and walked out of my bedroom to find Dad in the kitchen, cooking pancakes, eggs, and bacon while listening to the radio. My stomach growled from the sweet, salty, and juicy, tasty mixture in the air.

"Mhmm, Dad, smells good."

"Oh really?"

"Yeah."

"Good, I'm glad it smells good to you,"

Then it suddenly got quiet between us, and Dad looked away from me and started to flip the bacon. But I kept looking straight at him. Come on, Dad, just talk to me. Even though I know what's going on with you, talk to me still so I know how you really feel and so you can be happy once again. After waiting a while, I finally got the guts to say, "Dad, look at me and tell me what's going on with you."

Dad looked at me with puppy-dog eyes and stopped flipping the bacon and turned toward me.

"Okay," he started, and I waited for him to finish. "I know I haven't been myself lately, but, um." Then he paused when the song "Old Man" by Neil Young came on. I noticed a twinkle in his eyes. He tried to look away so I couldn't see that he was starting to cry. But that didn't stop me from getting him to talk. No siree, it didn't.

I smiled at him and said, "It's okay, Dad, I know." For once he looked straight at me. Tears were rushing down his cheeks, and he tried to wipe them off before I saw, but I did, and that was just fine with me. He let out a long, shaky breath and said, "Oh, come here, boy." He wrapped his arms around me and gave me a big, tight hug. I felt a little blue myself when Dad whispered, "I love you, son." He tightened his grip.

"I love you too, Dad."

Then I heard a door open, and Matt came peeking out from the hallway. "Hey, don't leave me out!" He walked up to me and put his arms around us.

"I want some hugs too."

Then the front door opened and Dan came in and said, "Hey, what's going on here?" Then the gang appeared behind him.

"I don't know," Mark said, "but I'm getting in on this action." He walked over to us, and the rest followed him, and they all got in on the group hug. It was kind of weird that Dad and I hugged, then everyone came out of nowhere, but it's okay, because I was just happy that our whole family was there at that moment, where a mixture of happy and sad emotions met together to create what is called a family. But that's just a weird way to explain it. It was even weirder to find Jessie sitting there, looking at us swaying back and forth. It was probably awkward for her mostly because she probably didn't know what to do. Like she didn't know if she should get in with us or what.

We smiled at her and started to cheer her on to come in this family group hug because right then and there, we knew that she was part of this family and would always be part of this crazy, loving, strange, uncontrollable family of joyfulness and wildness. Which she was pretty stubborn about getting in the group hug, but she gave up and rolled her eyes and jumped in. Then Dad looked down at her and said, "Welcome to the family, Jessie," with a great big smile on his face.

And the next thing I know is after 182 dates and three years, Jess and Dan are more in love than ever. You know the XOs kind of thing. And like I said in the beginning of the story, Jess and Dan are getting married, and boy, Dan's been stressing out about a lot of things. Like the wedding going badly, him messing up, or Jessie refusing to marry him, which will never happen because, like I said before, they're too in love to break up.

I told him Jessie would never leave him for the whole world. That made him feel a little better, I guess, but he sighed and said, "I know, but I don't know more than half of her family, Mike." He tightened his tie. "And that's what scares me, what if they don't like me?" Now I couldn't say anything about that because I only knew less than half of her whole family, so I sat there and let him speak his mind. "I don't want Jessie to think I'm having second thoughts or not knowing what I want or I don't know."

Matt gave him a funny look and said, "Are you having second thoughts about the wedding?"

Dan gave him that same funny look. "What, no. I said I don't want her to think I'm having second thoughts, Matt." He started to fix himself up. "I promise you I'm not, it's just a lot of pressure when you're getting married to the woman of your dreams. Not to say it was bad enough proposing to her, and you all know how that went."

"Yep, we know," Bradley said, chuckling. "And it went horribly wrong. I'm still surprised she said yes." Then he burst out laughing. Till John pushed him out of his chair.

"Shut up, you little shithead, can't you see it's bad enough that he is already stressed out about the wedding?" He walked over to Dan. "Don't listen to him, Danny, he doesn't know what it's like to be in a relationship with somebody or to get married to someone," he said as he put a hand on Dan's shoulder. "Now just keep it cool."

"How in the world can I keep it cool when there's, like, two hundred people staring at me."

John rolled his eyes and said, "There's not going to be two hundred people staring at you. There's going be, like, a hundred people staring at you." He put his hands on his hips.

"That's still a lot of eyeballs looking at you, John," Dan said, putting on his suit jacket.

Then Jessie's brother Jason came in with a big smile on his face and said, "You boys ready?"

Dan whispered with a light smile, "Ready as I'll ever be."

He smiled. "Hey, no pressure, buddy, just stay calm."

Dan looked at him and said, "I'll try my best."

"Really?" John said.

"What? It sounds better coming from the bride's brother."

"Well, what about the bride's brother-in-law, gosh damn."

"Wow! Language!" Dan said with a bit of sass.

"I meant the kind of dam, like dam in a lake or river, not the bad language damn."

"Oh, okay," Dan said kind of exhaustedly. Then we all started arguing about that along the way to the altar.

Now, after all the bumps in the road and all the dates they went on, Dan and Jessie were finally making it official. Which took long enough. I sat there, standing by the altar with the gang and Dan. I looked at Dan, who was standing next to the preacher. I could tell he was still stressing out by the way he was rubbing his hands as Jessie walked down the aisle with her big brother Joshua holding her arm. But when they got to Dan and the preacher, I heard Joshua say, "Now you better take good care of my little sister. She means the world to me, okay."

Jessie got up next to where Dan was standing. Dan smiled and said "I promise" as he took Jessie's small hands.

Then Joshua said, "And stop stressing out, it's not going to do you any good. Trust me, it didn't help me at all."

Jessie looked at Dan. "You'll be fine, don't worry, I'll be right here," she said as she faced him.

Then Dan let out that big breath of relief. They got started on their vows, then I began to think how great it had been these last three and half years of them being together. What will happen next? Will they think about having kids? I'm ready to be an uncle anytime now. Even though I wouldn't be able to go to their house for a while, I'll still be excited to be an uncle to a nephew or niece or both.

After the preacher said "You may kiss the bride," they began to kiss, until a little boy yelled "Eww!" who was sitting next to Matt and his girlfriend, and Mark yelled "Right there with you, buddy!" There was a short laughter in the crowd, and everyone started to clap their hands and cheer. After the wedding, we went to the after-party, and everyone was dancing to the song "Crazy Love" by Van Morriso. Blake, who actually came to the wedding, was crying probably for the first time in a long time. Oh, brother, I thought to myself as a smirk climbed up my cheek.

Sitting there looking at Dan and Jessie, with big smiles on their faces as they slow danced looking into each other's eyes, made me realize that Jess and Dan don't love each other because of the way they looked.

They love each other for who they were and who they are now, inside and out. Not for what they are or what they did or for their money, but for the way they can trust each other without feeling like they're being lied to, but even if they were lied to, they would find a way to make it up because of the sweet sorrows they had and always will have for each other, and the ripe and unripe memories, good and bad, could never unsweeten their sorrows that they had for each other. How could it ever? I mean, it wasn't all about the money, but it was about how much they love each other. That's when I knew that Jessie Herman was now part of our family. So now we all can say, "Welcome to the family, Jessie!" And to think, it all started on a field where we played football, where a big man fell in front of a little woman with a big heart who made our family even bigger and gave us one heck of an adventure together.

Now, what is love? Love is a gift that if given to someone, it should be cherished, not wasted by hatred. Because love is a kind of gift that is hard to find and even hard to receive. So if someone embraces their love to you in a compassionate way, you should revere it because you'll probably never find another love like them. But that's not all what love is or how it can be used. Love is what makes a family a family because love is thicker than blood, sweeter than a friendship, stronger than a gang held together by chains, and is more forgiving than anyone. So promise me you will never, ever forget who your family is and how much they love you. Because it might come as a surprise to some people, but a family is something you can forgive but never forget, because a family are the people who've been there for you most of your life, at the hardest times and the good times and have helped you when you really need it. Now a family isn't always blood, okay. But most of the time it is the people who've been there for you and helped you and always tell you they love you. So never,

ever think that the people who raise you hate you or don't care about you, because they do; you're just growing up too fast for them, and if you grow faster, they're getting older faster, and there's no stopping old age. And one day you'll be in their place, and they don't want you to be in that place.

They want you to stay young just a little longer so they can live a little bit longer with you. 'Cause one day they won't be there for you to help you. So please treat your family with respect because the really do love you. Well, you guys have been a great crowd. I can't wait to tell you about the next adventure of our growing family. But for right now, stay true to yourself and kind to others. Till next time, my friends.

ABOUT THE AUTHOR

Zoe F. Quintero was thirteen years old, going to fourteen in April, when she started to write the book *Welcome to the Family, Jessie*. She wrote this book because ever since she started middle school, she has wanted to write something that people can learn something from or have an understanding of. So she decided to write a book and try to get it published around her birthday. This book is mostly about family, with some comedy, and has a good amount of romance in it too. But it's mostly about family and knowing what it means to be part of the family and that blood isn't always family but the people around you who've been there for you when you need them the most, and the people that take care of you are also part of your family and forgiving you for your mistakes. At first she didn't know how to really tell you what it was about. She was going for just a plain old romance story, but as she read it, it sounded a little more about family than anything she was going for.

CPSIA information can be obtained
at www.ICGtesting.com
Printed in the USA
FFHW022031190719
53734483-59426FF